In the roadside towns, the wizards picked up stories and rumors. One man told how frost formed on the windows at night, though it was only the middle of September. There were no scrolls or intricate fern leaves, no branching overlaid starclusters; instead people saw seasick wavy lines, disturbing maps that melted into each other and always seemed on the verge of some recognizable but fearful shape. At dawn the frost melted, always in the same way: At first two eyeholes formed, and then a long steam-lipped mouth that spread and ate up the wandering white picture. . . . Voices rose from empty wells, and men locked their doors at dusk.

But Prospero and Roger Bacon refused to be daunted, although their road would take them to an end that mirrored their beginning, to uncover the power of

THE FACE IN THE FROST

THE FACE IN THE FROST

by JOHN BELLAIRS

Illustrated by Marilyn Fitschen

ACE FANTASY BOOKS
NEW YORK

This Ace Fantasy Book contains the complete
text of the original hardcover edition.
It has been completely reset in a typeface
designed for easy reading, and was printed
from new film.

THE FACE IN THE FROST

An Ace Fantasy Book / published by arrangement with
Macmillan Publishing Co., Inc.

PRINTING HISTORY
Ace edition / December 1978
Sixth printing / July 1984

ISBN: 0-441-22530-6

Ace Fantasy Books are published by The Berkley Publishing Group,
200 Madison Avenue, New York, New York 10016.
PRINTED IN THE UNITED STATES OF AMERICA

To the Memory of my Mother

PROLOGUE

Prospero and Roger Bacon, the two main characters in a story that seems crammed with wizards, were wizards. They knew seven different runic alphabets, could sing the *Dies Irae* all the way through to the end, and knew what a Hand of Glory was. Though they could not make the moon eclipse, they could do some very striking lightning effects and make it look as though it might rain if you waited long enough.

The two large domains mentioned in this tale were always known simply as the North Kingdom and the South Kingdom. No attempt was ever made to unite them, and the Brown River always remained the boundary. Even the maintenance and garrisoning of the two great circular forts at the mouth of the river had to be split rigidly between the kingdoms—Northerners guarded the northern fort, Southerners the southern one—though the forts had only one purpose—to keep out invaders from across the sea. The North Kingdom was split, very early in its history, into seven lesser kingdoms, whose kings met once a year on the Feasting Hill, which was in the center of a small, roughly circular plot of ground that touched all their borders, though it did not belong to any one ruler. At this harvest festival the High King was elected: he was usually one of the seven kings, but this was not necessary; his term was one year, and could be extended in case of war. He was given a standing army of ten thousand horsemen, but he would have been powerless without the consent of the heptarchs, as the seven lesser kings were known, since any two of them could field an army greater than his. Besides, the High King was forced to leave his own domain in the hands of a temporary ruler (usually his chief steward, who became for the time a heptarch) and reign at the beautiful, but defenseless, palace on the Feasting Hill. His army was solely for use in defending the borders and—rarely—for waging war against a rebellious Northern king. In the latter case, a council of war would be called and the kings would decide whether the situation was grave enough to require action against one of their own number. Civil war was rare, but when it did come the devastation was so great that it took generations for the North to recover.

The history of the South Kingdom was stranger and much more chaotic. If you looked at a map of the South made in Prospero's time, you would think it was a badly done and rather fussy abstract painting, or the palette of a demented artist. You would see blotches within splotches within wavy circles; you would see shapes like ladyfingers, like stars, like dumbbells, and like creeping dry rot. All this was the fault of Godwin I (Longbeard), the first King of All the South, and the last to hold any real power. He divided up the kingdom among his sons, and they did likewise, and so on. Primogeniture was never established, so eventually the South became an indescribable conglomeration of duchies, earldoms, free cities, minor kingdoms, independent bishoprics, and counties. These little worlds were often the size of small farms, though they might be named the Grand Union of the Five Counties, or the Duchy of Irontree-Dragonrock. Each of these petty potentates coined his own money and levied troops; all were vaguely obligated to the King of All the South, a powerless ruler who got the title by beating all opponents at the annual tournament held in Roundcourt, the chief city of the South. Seldom could a chieftain gather enough support for anything the size of a civil war, but there was constant feuding, bickering, and bullying.

Prospero lived in the South Kingdom and never, as far as I know, held public office. He stayed at home a great deal, and his trips to other places in the North and South were made on odd occasions and (sometimes) by still odder modes of travel. The route might be wildly irregular, because he wanted to see friends or visit curious things, like plague fountains, or rocks that made funny noises in the wind. This accounts for the fact that he knew more about some places far up north than he knew about places ten miles from his home. Roger Bacon, who spent most of his time in England, was more familiar with the border country between the North and the South than Prospero was. Both of them had used mirrors to visit or look at other times and places; this naturally affected their speech, their mannerisms, and (God knows) the character of Prospero's house.

ONE

Several centuries (or so) ago, in a country whose name doesn't matter, there was a tall, skinny, straggly-bearded old wizard named Prospero, and not the one you are thinking of, either. He lived in a huge, ridiculous, doodad-covered, trash-filled two-story horror of a house that stumbled, staggered, and dribbled right up to the edge of a great shadowy forest of elms and oaks and maples. It was a house whose gutter spouts were worked into the shape of whistling sphinxes and screaming bearded faces; a house whose white wooden porch was decorated with carved bears, monkeys, toads, and fat women in togas holding sheaves of grain; a house whose steep gray-slate roof was capped with a glass-enclosed, twisty-copper-columned observatory. On the artichoke dome of the observatory was a weather vane shaped like a dancing hippopotamus; as the wind changed, it blew through the nostrils of the hippo's hollow head, making a whiny snarfling sound that fortunately could not be heard unless you were up on the roof fixing slates.

Inside the house were such things as trouble antique dealers' dreams: a brass St. Bernard with a clock in its side, and a red tongue that went in and out with the ticks as the tail wagged; a five-foot iron statue of a tastefully draped lady playing a violin (the statue was labeled "Inspiration"); mahogany chests covered with leering cherub faces and tiger mouths that bit you if you put your finger in the wrong place; a cherrywood bedstead with a bassoon carved into one of the fat headposts, so that it could be played as you lay in bed and meditated; and much more junk; and deep closets crammed with things that peered out of the darkness off the edges of shelves, frightening the wits out of the wizard as he poked around looking for jars of mandrake root or dwarf hair in aspic. In the long, high living room—heated by a wide-mouthed green-stone fireplace—were the usual paraphernalia of a practicing wizard: alembics, spiraling copper coils, alcohol lamps—all burping, sputtering, and glurping as red, blue, purple, and green liquids boiled, dripped, or just slurched uncertainly in their containers. On a shelf over the experiment table was the inevitable skull, which the wizard put there to remind him of death, though it usually reminded him that he needed to go to the dentist. One wall of the room was lined with bookshelves, and on them you could find titles such as *Six Centuries of English Spells*, *Nameless Horrors and What to Do About Them*, *An Answer for Night-Hags*, and, of course, the dreaded *Krankenhammer* of Stefan Schimpf, the mad cobbler of Mainz.

The four long casement windows on the east wall of the

living room opened onto Prospero's forest-bordered garden, an unpruned tangle of forsythia, rose, and lilac bushes split up by a few matted green paths. In the middle of the garden was a small clearing with stone benches and wicker lawn chairs; this park had a fountain, in the center of which a potbellied marble satyr stared mindlessly into an empty cup, as water gushed out of his ears. On summer mornings, Prospero would often sit in this weedy jungle, memorizing spells and watching the birds as they circled in confusion around the gables, pinnacles, and gargoyles that stared out in all directions from his improbable home.

But on a hot, oppressive morning one August, Prospero stayed in bed till almost noon. He was not playing the bassoon, but he *was* thinking, lying there on his back with his hands folded on his chest. Finally, with an effort, he got up and went to the window, opened it, and stood looking down at the ground for quite some time. With a little shrug he turned away, and was poking around in a bureau drawer when a voice snapped at him:

"Do you think the roof will fall in on us today? Did the frost hurt your stinkweed?"

That was the magic mirror, a competent but somewhat sarcastic mirror in a heavy gilt frame. When the magician was not trying to get something out of it, it was given to tuneless humming and crabby remarks.

"I don't know what you're talking about," growled Prospero as he hunted for his toothbrush.

"You know very well what I mean," said the mirror in an unpleasant tone. "What's all this staring at the ceiling and thinking? Have you discovered a cure for mangy eyebrows?"

"I may discover a cure for talkative pieces of plate glass," said the wizard, grinding his teeth.

"Boorish threats," said the mirror. "By the way, if you step over here now, you can view Aurungabad, as seen from the ruins of the palace of Aurungzebe."

"How nice," muttered Prospero, and he disappeared into the bathroom with a balding toothbrush clenched in his fist.

A little later, as Prospero was soaking in a large porcelain tub with eagle-claw legs, the mirror began to sing:

> *"O-over-head the moon is SCREEEEAMING,*
> *Whi-ite as turnips on the Rhine . . ."*

Most of the time, the mirror's singing voice might have been compared with that of a tubercular reed organ; but when it hit high notes, Prospero thought of children with long nails scraping on blackboards. So it was not surprising that the wizard soon emerged from the bathroom, wet and dripping and wrapped in a yellow-damask towel that looked like a Byzantine cope.

"All right," he said quietly. "Let's see what we can see."

The wizard peered deep into the fathomless depths of the murky mirror, and when the swirling mists cleared, he found himself watching a 1943 game between the Chicago Cubs and the New York Giants. The Cubs were behind 16-0 in the eighth inning.

Prospero stood silently watching for a few seconds. Then, with an evil grin, he produced from behind his back a large cake of soap. "Now watch it, whiskers," said the mirror, alarmed. "Don't you dare . . . Ak Hoog! Glph . . . Hphfmphpph!"

Prospero scribbled wildly on the mirror with the cake of soap, signed his name with a flourish, and went downstairs, chuckling.

But not even his victory over the cranky mirror could

help Prospero to shake off the uncertain fear that hung in the still, heavy air of that August day. Something was coming, and he would have given his hat to know what it was. In the meantime, he fribbled away the day with mindless tasks like cleaning the ashpit of the fireplace and raising the ghosts of flowers. From a square bottle marked "Essential Salts," Prospero poured a few green crystals into a white ceramic dish; when he had mumbled some words over the bowl, a pink and green cloud began to ascend from the shimmering translucent pebbles. Before long, a definite shape appeared.

"Carnations," said the wizard disgustedly. "Phooey."

He fanned at the uninteresting specter until it blew out the window in a long sickly streamer of colored smoke. Then, with a distracted air, he walked to a carved lectern that held a large, unlabeled folio volume. It was a thick, dog-eared book in a cracked, brown leather cover, and its blue-ruled pages were filled with the wizard's florid script; on some pages were pentacles, pentagrams, and doodles, these latter being usually pictures of bearded patriarchs, pharaohs, and King Louis XI of France, who, as far as Prospero was concerned, looked like this:

On some pages were spells set to music: the curious words, split up into syllables, wandered through bars of badly drawn square notes. He selected one of these incantations

5

and began to chant in a loud, wailing voice. All the clocks in the house suddenly went off at once, though it was only three-twenty; the copper pots hanging in the kitchen clanged and whanged against each other; and a couple of the wizard's books fell off their shelves with a clump. But nothing else happened. Prospero slammed the magic book shut and slumped into an overstuffed chair. He fumbled in his smoking stand for his pipe and tobacco.

"I learned that spell fifty years ago," he mumbled as he lit his pipe. "And I still don't know what it's for."

Around six o'clock a dark greenish storm-twilight descended, though the sun was not due to set for two hours. Prospero got up and walked out the back door into this unnatural dusk; in the yard behind the house no birds could be seen or heard; the leaves of the trees hung like carved ornaments; and even the splashing of the fountain was strangely muted. The slates of the roof were a flat gray, and the thick-piled clouds seemed to press down on the turreted house. Prospero went back inside and decided to prepare dinner for himself. He pottered about in the kitchen in an attempt at a cheerful manner, whistling bits of tunes like "Lilliburlero" and "The Piper of Dundee." But his whistling died away as he suddenly thought, with inexplicable dread, that he would have to go down into the cellar for a pitcher of ale. Now a grown man—especially one who is a wizard— is not supposed to be afraid of going to the cellar at night. But, though he loved the strong brown ale that aged in oozing vats in his dark cool basement, Prospero would (this time) have just as soon done without.

"This is silly," he said to himself. "You are a coward and a lumphead." He lit a tall, twisty beeswax candle and grabbed a fat pewter pitcher from the nail where it hung.

The cellarway was dark and musty-smelling, and a damp breeze blew from a window that must have been left open. Prospero, moving along cautiously in the wavering yellow light, passed shelves of cobwebbed jelly jars and dusty overturned steins with inscriptions in strange blue letters. Overhead were the floor beams of the house, split logs with the furrowed black bark still on them. When he reached the great rounded shapes of the beer kegs, Prospero stuck the candle into a wooden wall socket and turned toward a heavy brassbound tun labeled "XXX Strong Ale." Setting the pitcher on a shelf just under the blocky wooden spigot, he turned the handle, and the ale gushed into the container with a tinny rising sound.

He looked absently around the cellar as he waited for the pitcher to fill, and suddenly his eye was caught by the fluttering of an old cloak hanging on a wooden peg. And in that instant Prospero got the odd notion that the cloak was not his, and might not be a cloak at all. He stared intently at it as the fluttering of the garment became more agitated. And then it turned to meet him. With empty flapping arms it floated across the cellar floor, swaying in a sickening nightmare rhythm. Prospero clenched his fist and felt his pulse beating in his palms; he fought the rising fear as the cloak flapped nearer, for with all his heart he did not want it close to him. As it closed the gap between them, all the spells against apparitions ran through his mind, but he had the queasy feeling that none of them would work. The thing was about six feet from him, its cold musty-cellar breath faintly brushing his face, when it simply stopped. The flapping arms dropped, and the gray cloak, or whatever it was, slumped into a ragged heap on the stone floor. Prospero stepped back nervously and stiffened as he felt a cold sensation. But when

7

he looked down he laughed abruptly, since he had stepped into the spreading brown pool of ale that was now sloshing and frothing over the sides of the pitcher. He shut off the spigot and leaned, trembling, against the barrel, his forehead pressing the fragrant wet wood. When he looked again at the place on the floor where the cloak had fallen, he was not surprised to see that there was nothing lying on the rough candlelit stone. The peg where the cloak had first hung was not there either.

As soon as he felt able to walk, Prospero grabbed up the brimming pitcher, snatched the candle from its sconce, and dashed up the creaking wooden stairs. When he got back to the kitchen he felt better, and, since ghostly cloaks should be common experience for a sorcerer, he felt a little ashamed. But when he closed his eyes, the scene in the cellar came back with all its inexplicable terror.

"Well," said Prospero to himself, "the thing to do is to keep my eyes open and eat my dinner."

Which he did, though he had hardly gotten halfway through his meal of cold roast beef, ale, and Cheshire cheese when the heavy hanging storm broke over the house with a long, splitting, plate-rattling crash. The thunder did not frighten Prospero half so much as his reaction to it, which was to shove his chair back and look quickly over his shoulder. For the next hour he was plagued by the strong, palpable feeling that someone was behind him. Even in his study, where he had pushed his big wing chair up against the paneled wall, he found that he could not read—the shadows that leaned out over the high-sided chair seemed more than shadows. He got up and went back to the kitchen, where he nervously finished his dinner as the rain swished and rattled at the diamond-paned window; he tried to play solitaire with an old oblong deck of tarot cards; and he finally settled in his wing chair again to read by the warm light of a squat, ruby-shaded oil lamp.

By nine o'clock the storm had passed over and crickets were chirping in the wet grass outside. Prospero found himself still edgy, and he was reading the same sentence about wood trolls for the third time when the doorbell rang. The bell was a small, tinkling silver toy with a chain pull, but just then it sounded like a rusty iron bourdon tolling in an empty church on a winter night. Prospero let the heavy volume he was holding slip to the floor with a loud dust-raising whump. He stared for several minutes at the half-open study door that led to the dark front hall. Finally, with a sudden resolute jerk, he stood up, crossed the room, and peered into the narrow vestibule. The linen-curtained square window in the front door threw a wavering yellow patch on the splintered floorboards, and the huddled shapes of picture frames, dressers, and coat trees leaned out from the walls. Staring intently at the blank yellow window, Prospero stepped into the hall and lurched into a massive mahogany coat tree. The tall spindled thing rocked on its warped base, and three or four umbrellas fell in the wizard's path with a swishing clatter. Shaken, but still relatively calm, he stepped over the scattered junk and got to the door, grasped the cold porcelain knob, and pulled. The swollen black door would not open at his first jerk, or at the second. On the third try it rattled suddenly inward and the chilly night air, smelling of cut grass and rain-drenched lilacs, blew gently into the hall. From the blistered white porch ceiling hung a square yellow-paned lantern, and around it mosquitoes, moths, and other night insects flittered and ticked. The tiny doorbell was still trembling on its rusty hook. No one was there.

Prospero stood under the lamp, staring out into the moonless night. At first he saw only vague shapes, some darker than others, but before long he became aware of a small figure standing halfway down the flagstone walk. As Prospero watched, the figure raised a threatening arm and spoke in a deep voice:

"Kill them all!"

At this Prospero did a strange thing. He began to smile. His long wrinkled face, which had been set in a tense frown, was now creased by a delighted grin.

"Kill who all?" he asked in an amused voice.

"All those blasted, pesty, nitty insects!" the figure roared. "If yellow light attracts moths the size of horse blankets, why don't you get a purple lamp or a green lamp? At least let me smash the one you have!"

Still grumping, the person on the walk came forward until he stood in the light. Prospero saw a short, burly, middle-aged man with a close-trimmed dark-red beard; the hair on his head was beginning to get gray, and it was hard to tell whether he was going bald or just wearing a badly overgrown tonsure. The monkish aspect was also suggested by a mud-splashed brown robe, over which a shiny rain slicker was thrown. But instead of sandals, the man wore scuffed brown walking boots. In one hand he held a dripping sou'wester rain hat, and in the other he held a long brass-tipped staff. A fat brown valise crouched at his feet, like an absurd and lumpy short-haired dog. It was Roger Bacon, one of Prospero's best friends and a pretty good sorcerer in his own right. He had been in the North Kingdom for the last three years, and before that he had been in England for three years. But you would have thought the two men had not seen each other in fifty years, the way they pounded each other on the back, bellowing wisecracks about falling hair and midriff bulge. When the welcoming uproar had subsided, Prospero stepped back and made a deep, comic bow.

"Welcome, noble friar! And when did you return from the land of ice and mist?"

"Just tonight. A fishing boat put me ashore on the coast, and I found my way here as well as I could. I got—"

Suddenly Roger looked up, because some movement near the porch ceiling caught his eye. A huge gray moth, at least two hand spans across, came flapping down from the shadows. It went straight for Prospero, and before he could raise his hand it had plastered itself against his face. Roger gave a sharp cry and rushed forward, shooing at the thing until it dropped to the floor with a light plop and an unpleasant rustling sound. But before Roger could step on it, the moth rose, dived once at his head, and then floated off into the night. The two men stared after it for a full minute, and when Roger turned to look at Prospero, he saw that his face was pale, even in the yellow light. And his hands were trembling.

"Look here," said Roger in a worried voice. "I wish you'd tell me what's going on. You're not normally scared of insects, but then that was no ordinary moth. I've never seen one like it."

Prospero sighed and rubbed at his face with both hands. "I'd tell you what was going on if I knew. I've never seen anything like it either. It smelled like a basement full of dusty newspapers. But the smell isn't the worst thing about it."

"That's true," said Roger, looking up at the porch lamp. "It never came close to me, and I was scared of it. Well, it's just more of what I felt when I got here two hours ago, and—"

Prospero stared at him. "Two hours ago! Why didn't you come in?"

Roger took a deep breath and let it out slowly. "As soon

as I came through the gate, I knew that something else was here, something that had nothing to do with you or your spells. So I poked around out here in the rain in hopes of catching the thing or at least finding out what it was."

"And did you find anything?"

"No. Out by the fountain I scared off something that might have been a dog, though it didn't look like one: It stood near the edge of the forest and stared at me for a moment, but when I threatened it with my staff, it ran away. There were sounds in the tall grass and in the bushes. All this in the wild rain, and your house all lit up. It was a bit like a dream I used to have as a child: I would be chased around and around the outside of my house by a tall, formless dark creature; every window in the house was brightly lit and yet I couldn't go in. Of course, I could have come into *your* house if I had wanted to. But I felt you were safe; the thing was outside."

"It had been inside," said Prospero grimly. And now it was Roger Bacon's turn to stare.

Prospero decided right then that a little false courage was needed—otherwise the two of them would spend the rest of the night looking in closets and under tables.

"Come on inside," he said. "The ghastly grimling is gone, at least for the time being, and we have a lot of talking to catch up on. It's getting chilly, so why don't you start a fire, and I'll go downstairs—" He paused and laughed. He was not frightened now and he was genuinely amused at himself. Roger, naturally, still looked puzzled. "Never mind," Prospero went on, "I'll explain later. Anyway, as I was saying, I'll go downstairs and get a bottle of good red wine and some of that hundred-year-old brandy you had the last time you were here. And we'll see what we can do to that large

Cheshire cheese in the kitchen. How does that sound?"

"Fine," said Roger, and he started to take off his heavy raincoat.

Before long the two of them were comfortably planted in two large, sagging easy chairs drawn up before a warm fire, which sometimes burned bright sea green or deep cobalt blue because of salts that Prospero had thrown onto the logs. Between the chairs was a small octagonal table holding a dusty green wine bottle, a rapidly diminishing half wheel of cheese, and a plate of crackers. Roger Bacon had been telling about some of his more notable successes in England, and now he began to tell, with equal delight, some stories about his more egregious failures.

". . . and so I went to work on a brazen head that was going to tell me how to encircle England with a wall of brass, to keep out marauding Danes and other riffraff. I think something went wrong when I didn't put enough yellow regulus of phosphorus in—or maybe there was too much astatine permanganate. Anyway, I got a head that was at least as talkative as your mirror . . ."

"I heard that!" yelled a voice from upstairs.

"You be quiet," shouted Prospero over his shoulder. "Why don't you go watch late movies or something?"

There was silence upstairs, followed shortly by the muffled sound of bird imitations.

"*Anyway*," Roger went on, munching a piece of cheese, "the head did talk a lot, but unlike your mirror it was deaf as a . . . as a . . ."

"Brass post?" put in Prospero helpfully.

"Yes," muttered Roger, giving him a dirty look. "You might say so. Well, I asked it how to make a brass wall to encircle England, and it said 'Hah?' *'Brass wall,'* I said, louder. *'B* as in Bryophyta . . . ' "

"Bryophyta?" Prospero asked.

"Yes," answered Roger testily, "mosses and liverworts."

"I hate liver," said Prospero.

"As well you might," said Roger in a quiet, despairing voice. "As well you might. But be that as it may, I spelled it out. *R* as in rotogravure process . . ." He waited, but Prospero, who was biting down hard on his pipe to keep from laughing, did not interrupt. ". . . *A* as in Anaxagoras, *S* as in Symplegades, and *S* as in Smead Jolley, the only baseball player in history to make four errors on a single played ball."

"And what did the head say?"

"It said 'Umpf,' or something like that, and then it started to rattle off a long formula, which I may have copied wrong. Or maybe the head didn't know what it was talking about. At any rate, when I chanted the formula the next day, down by the seashore, I heard a sound like crumhorns and shawms, and behold! All of England was encircled with an eight-foot-high wall of *Glass!*"

"Glass? Plain, ordinary glass?"

"Yes, and not very good glass at that. Paper-thin and full of bubbles and pocks. The first boatload of Vikings that came over after the wall went up turned around and went back, because it was a sunny day and the wall glittered wonderfully. But the next day, when they came back, it was cloudy. One of them gave the wall a little tap with an ax, and it went tinkle, tinkle, and now there is a lot of broken glass on the beach. Not long after that I was asked to leave."

Prospero could not think of anything adequate to say, so he suggested that they break out the brandy and cigars.

They talked on into the night, and the large candle in

15

the corner, shaped like the head of a mournful monk, got
sadder and sadder looking. But as the candle got scowlier,
the two men became more delighted and talkative, so that
Prospero finally felt up to telling Roger about the cloak in
the cellar. Roger listened with a concerned and sometimes
frightened look on his face, and when the story was over he
put his brandy glass down and waited a bit before he spoke.

"You don't mention the moth, but I suppose that neither
of us has to dot such a large *i*. Has anything else happened?"

Prospero nodded. "Last night I dreamed that I was still
in bed, but wide awake, staring at something near the foot
of my bed. I stared for a long while at the vague shape, and
I gradually made out the form of an old man standing there.
When he came forward into the moonlight, I could see that
he was watching me with a scornful smile—it was a cruel,
cynical face, the arrogant face of a man who is secure in
some superior power or knowledge. Without saying anything, he went to the window, which was bright with the
light of a full moon. And then he began to write on the
windowpane with his index finger, and it seemed to me that
each stroke of his finger cut into the glass like a diamond.
For some reason, although the words glowed with a silver
light, I couldn't get any meaning out of the writing. I
strained my eyes and stared, but it all seemed like nonsense.
Then the old man turned to me and said, 'Can you read what
I have written?' When I said that I could not, he laughed a
low, mocking laugh and his whole face contorted in a contemptuous sneer. 'That is unfortunate,' he said, in a cold
voice. 'You will suffer because of your ignorance.'

"At that point I woke up. The room was bright with
moonlight, but of course there were no words on the window
and, as far as I could tell, there was no one in the room. So I

went back to sleep again, and I'm not sure how long I slept, but I was awakened by the sound of someone tapping on my window. It was a sharp, metallic sound, not like someone rapping with his knuckles, and I sat up with a start. When I looked at the window, which is not very far from my bed, I saw that there was a large bird outside on the sill. And a second later I saw that it was not an ordinary bird. It was skeletal. The gray light was shining through its rib cage and its eyeholes; it was pecking at the pane and clattering its horrible black wings against my window. I was suddenly seized with the fear that it would break through the glass at

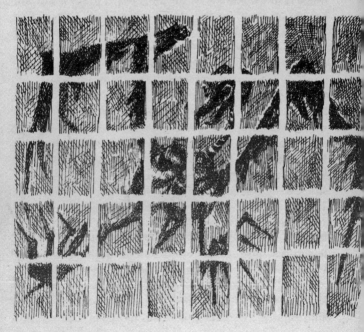

any minute and get in, and I jumped out on the opposite side of the bed. I got hold of my staff, which was leaning against the wall near the bed, and I muttered some kind of charm, I forget what. It didn't work, but a minute or two later the bird gave an awful scraping cry and fell over backward, off the sill."

Roger opened his mouth to say something, but Prospero raised his hand.

"I know what you're going to say. But the bird was *not* in a dream. I sat there on the edge of the bed for some time after the thing vanished, but I finally did get some sleep. The next morning—this morning—I looked to see if the bird had left any mark on the ground where it fell. It had. The grass was crushed down in one spot under my window. It wasn't a dream, and these things—the bird, the moth, and the cloak—are not just apparitions."

"I don't see what you mean."

"Roger, you know as well as I do that apparitions, evil or otherwise, are abroad in the world. You have put them down with incantations and so have I. But *these* things were tangible—they were real in a way that a ghost is not. Have you ever gotten close enough to an apparition to try to touch it?"

Roger thought for a minute. "Well," he said, "I once had to put to rest the ghost of an old woman who was haunting a village south of here. She had been a witch, and her power to return came from a little wooden charm she had hidden under the floor of her house. I found it and decided to burn it in the town square—with the proper ceremonies, of course. When I set fire to the amulet, she appeared and rushed at me with her arms raised. She had long hooked nails and looked as though she wanted to scratch my eyes out."

"And what did you feel? Did she touch you?"

"She passed right through me. There was a cold breath, but not much else."

"Exactly. But *these* things could be felt and smelled. That evil gray cloak never touched me, but it must have been as palpable as the others. It had a dead smell about it, and it made a swishing sound as it moved across the floor. And there was something else, something that you must have felt when the moth appeared. You said that you were scared by the moth, even though it didn't come near you. Do you know why you were scared?"

Roger looked nervously around the dark room.

"I felt that there was someone there. I felt the power of some incredibly hateful will, a human will that wanted to kill you. And just before the moth flew away, I felt the will grow fainter."

"Not quite ready," said Prospero with a sour smile. "Whoever he is, he can't do what he wants to do just yet. *If* there is such a he, that is. We may be wrong about all this. Anyway, we ought to talk about something else. There's nothing more maddening than empty speculation."

Roger sat up in his chair. "Good Lord! I had forgotten all about the notes I brought you. On the book."

"Book?" said Prospero.

Roger looked at him in exasperation. "Yes, book! Remember? Just before I left for England you asked me to trace that book, the one written in the cipher that no one had been able to crack. Well, you were right. The book has been in England and may still be there, for all I know, though I couldn't locate it. It had been in several castle libraries and was mainly thought of as a curiosity. Most of the old scholars I talked to thought the book must be some kind of practical joke, an elaborate sport. It made its way from one library to another because people borrowed it and never returned it. Not that anyone tried to get it back. No one in England took the book seriously, as far as I know, except one monk at Glastonbury Abbey. He has been dead for about fifty years now, but I found his notebooks under a pile of old papers in the abbey's archives. When you read what he has written, you may think that he was a little crazy. But I don't think so. Here, let me get the papers for you. I couldn't bring his actual notes, but I copied out everything pertaining to the book."

Roger got up and went to the hallway, where he fumbled about in his raincoat for a while. When he came back he was holding a bundle of rain-spotted foolscap sheets that were covered on both sides with his neat uncial script. Prospero refilled the brandy glasses, and he had just risen from his chair to look for his watch when a small marble clock high up on a dark shelf near the ceiling struck two. Not *bong-bong*, but *clunk-clunk*, since Prospero had stuffed the bells with paper to keep them from waking him up. When the muffled striking had finished, two wooden doors opened in the front of the clock and a small brass cannon rolled out. The spring-action barrel fired two metal pellets which flew across the room into the open mouth of a bust of Aristotle. The philosopher's eyes blinked red twice as the pellets went down his throat. *Gulp-gulp, ping-ping.* Roger stood staring at the spectacle.

"I do not think, Prospero," he said, "that one should attribute a very high degree of reality to your house."

"That clock is altogether too real," said Prospero. "I think I will have to stuff Aristotle's mouth with paper."

"You might try not winding up the clock," said Roger.

"Oh, my no!" said Prospero, deadpanning. "What would the clock think?"

The two men sat down again in the easy chairs. Prospero had brought a large floor candelabrum from the other room, and he had placed it between the two chairs. Now he began to read by the wavering shadowy light. He mumbled the first few lines of the first page to himself and looked up.

"This seems to be a very thorough description of the book. Is it from a catalogue of some sort?"

"Yes," said Roger. "The monk kept a descriptive list of all his books. Most of the entries are very brief and limited to standard descriptive terms, but this note is quite elaborate, and it certainly goes beyond the kind of thing you'd expect to find in a book list. The rest of the material you have there I copied from a diary he kept. I didn't include anything that did not pertain to the book. At first there are just a few scattered notes, but later he writes about the book obsessively. You will see why."

"You *do* know how to arouse curiosity," said Prospero, smiling. "Why don't I read this aloud? I hate long silences as much as you do, and we both enjoy being read to."

"Very well," said Roger, sitting back. "Anyway, I haven't read the thing since I was in the archives at Glastonbury. Read on."

Prospero began to read in a slow, matter-of-fact voice.

" 'Item 1036. Small quarto volume in vellum-covered boards. No markings on back or front cover or on spine. Little sign of wear. Contains 73 parchment leaves. Writing on both sides of leaves. Colored drawings in margins, small woodcuts used for initial letters, and some full-page woodcuts. Curious dolphin cross on last page. Bookplate on inside front cover. This latter has been defaced by some crisscross slashes probably made with a pen, but I can make out the design, which is this:'" Prospero found himself looking at a macabre heraldic device.

"Even though it's my drawing of his drawing," said Roger, "it's probably accurate. And it's familiar too, though I can't think why."

Prospero nodded. "I feel the same way. Well, let's go on. The book appears to be written in a cipher, though I cannot even make out the alphabet that is used. The writing is neat and flowing, and there seem to be words and word groups. There is something vaguely disturbing about the writing. The decorations are similarly odd and much more unsettling. The flowers drawn in the margins are minutely detailed, though they correspond to no flowers that I have ever seen, either in life or in my herb-books. Some flowers have men and women rising from them. Woodcuts used for initial letters are executed with skill. One shows a lighted window in a moonlit tower. A figure in the window, hunched over a lectern. A similar cut shows the scholar at his desk before an open book. A shadowed figure, presumably a friend, looks over his shoulder. One full-page woodcut shows (I imagine) the Witch of Endor. Certainly there are "gods ascending from the earth." The witch's back is to us and she is thrown into silhouette by the light of a fire. She holds a rod. The spirits, which are crawling out of the fire, look like horribly emaciated men. Some are on their knees begging, some are trying to flee, and one is crawling toward the witch with a look that gave me a bad dream the other night. Another full-page cut shows a man who has apparently just been awakened. He is in a nightgown and he holds a candle. Again, the face is away from us, for he looks toward a large open window. The light, or something about the drawing, is incredibly well done, making the window a terrifying black hole. Anything might crawl through it. Not that there are shapes in the window. It seems absolutely dark. I have contemplated burning this woodcut but I cannot do it. Twice I have awakened at night to find myself in the situation of the figure in the picture. Without a candle, but in bright moonlight. Once I woke up and found that I was unfastening the latch on my bedroom window. I have never been a sleep-walker before. God save me from a moonless night!' "

Prospero shuddered. "Even reading about this is horrible! Did anything happen to the poor man?"

"No . . . well, that is to say, he was not dragged off by dark creatures. But he—oh, read on! The diary is next."

Prospero continued:

" '*October 15:* Found an interesting-looking book in the library today. I asked the abbot if he would let me have it for my own collection in my laboratory, and he said yes. It appears to be in a strange language, and it may deal with magic.

" 'November 28: I must find time to study that new book; I fear my lack of training in languages will hinder me.

" 'January 21: I have been trying to unlock the cipher of this strange book. Having exhausted my supply of cryptographic manuals, I am sending to London for more. The writing looks as though it could be translated. That is, it is suggestive of some meaning.

" 'February 3: The new books are no help. I am going to give up trying to interpret this piece of nonsense. It has taken up far too much of my time. After all, it may be in a language I do not know. But then, why does it seem so meaningful?

" 'February 17: I will give this damnable book one last try. To the devil with all manuals! I should be able to solve it with my native wits.

" 'February 18: I stayed up all night, and toward morning, when the letters were twisting and squirming before my eyes, I found that the first two lines made sense. Laudate Dominum! All that is required, it seems, is concentration. It seems to be the beginning of an incantation of some sort. This has been a bitter winter. Wolves were howling last night in a grove of trees a few hundred yards from the abbey. I could see their eyes as I stood in my window.

" 'February 20: I have asked the abbot to excuse me from prayers for a few days so that I might finish something that will, I am sure, be for the greater glory of God. He consented, but reluctantly, and made a needlessly unpleasant remark about my haggard appearance. He has not wrestled with Powers and Principalities.

" '*March 13:* It has taken incredible concentration, but I have finished the first incantation. I assume it to be complete, since the next line is indented and begins with an ornamental capital. Tonight I will try the spell and see what it brings.

" '*March 14:* At first I was horribly disappointed. I chanted the words but nothing happened. However, I soon came to see that one has to want something specific to happen. I decided that the best thing would be to close my eyes and see what image formed. I saw many things, but one picture kept recurring: the snowy field outside my window, and in the middle of it one gray wolf. (No doubt this was the result of what I mentioned in my note of February 18.) I chanted the words again and went to my window. It was ten o'clock at night, a three-quarters-full moon was in the sky, and in the snow I saw a wolf staring up at me. In that instant I realized that I had *made* him, and that I could keep him there only by intense concentration. The moment my brain began to grow tired, the wolf began to shimmer and fade into the snow. When I ran outside I saw that the creature had left tracks. I have done what Tiresias, Simon Magus, Arbaces, and all the sibyls could not do.' "

Prospero dropped the papers into his lap. The two men stared at each other for a long time.

"Well," said Prospero at last, "I thought we were changing the subject when we started to read this thing."

"So did I," said Roger. "Fool that I am! I didn't notice the connection till you read it just now. This gives added significance to some things that happened later. Read on and you will see what I mean."

Prospero picked up the papers again.

" '*March 15:* The wolf will not obey my commands, though I can hold him here for upwards of an hour. I must read more. The abbot will not allow me to have my meals brought here. I spoke to him sharply, and he accused me of experimenting with black magic. I said that he spoke without knowledge, and quoted Job to him. He stared at me in wonder, and, I think, in fear. I expected him to ask me to kneel and beg forgiveness, but he hurried away.

"'*March 17:* More success with the control of the wolf. I have translated three whole paragraphs now. The intense study is affecting my nerves. I constantly think that someone is plucking at my sleeve. When I turn around there is no one there. And last night I dreamed that something dead lay alongside me in my bed. I woke up in terror and thought I heard something strike the floor. When I went to the window I saw the wolf. He had come unbidden; I do not know why.

"'*March 20:* Quarreled with the abbot again today. It seems very strange that he is opposed to what I am doing. Now that we speak of witchcraft, I wonder who *his* master is?

"'*March 28:* I cannot get beyond the third paragraph. Could it be that the rest of the book is untranslatable? I lack will power. Told the abbot that I would not obey his evil command.

"'*April 7:* It seems that the next paragraph is not an incantation at all, but a set of directives. Prerequisites for further action. I cannot believe that such demands need to be met, so I will simply continue to the next spell.

"'*April 23:* The words have fought me fiercely, but I am ready now. I think the "instructions" were interpolated by a madman.'"

Here Roger interrupted. "The next entry—the last one, as you see—has no date. The original page from the diary was torn out, crumpled, and thrown into the fire. Someone rescued it and stuck it back into the book, but the date was burned away."

Prospero read:

" 'I have smashed my bottles and retorts, and I have given the book to an old fisherman—a foreigner, but a good man—who promised me that he would drop it into the deepest part of the sea. How can I tell what has happened? I spoke the words I had learned, and suddenly the whole room began to waver and drift like smoke. I felt as if I could put my hand through the table and the walls. I saw everything as through murky water. The floor pitched like a deck, but with difficulty I got to the window. The wolf was out there on the grass, closer than ever before, but beside him was a man in a monk's robe. The cowl was thrown back, but I could not see his features through the shimmering air. Then his face grew impossibly large and came near, and I saw that it was mine—my face as it might be after a year in the grave. A voice, a dry insect voice, harsh and cracked, whispered, *"Give me the book."* I clutched the book to my chest and fell down to the floor, which was now like smoking, bubbling water. I could see through to the ground and there was no roof above me, and I was sinking with that awful rotted face hovering over me. I fainted, and when I awoke, the solid stone floor of my study was under me again. The book was there in my arms undamaged. What I did with it I have written above, and I swear to God that what I have written is true. The abbot has forgiven me, and I am to make a pilgrimage soon, *quia peccavi nimis.* I will take up my studies again when I feel able to."

Prospero sighed and folded up the notes. "Only one thing remains for me to ask, and I'm almost afraid to ask it," he said.

"I know what you mean," said Roger with a tense smile. "Yes, I did bring a sample of the book's script with me." He reached into his pocket and brought out a small wrinkled card. "This is in the monk's own handwriting. Is it the writing on your window?"

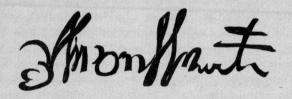

Prospero stared at the card, crumpled it slowly, and pressed his fist to his eyes. Then, standing up suddenly, he threw the wad across the room. It dropped neatly into the trumpet mouth of a potbellied brass spittoon.

"Come on," said Prospero, as he pulled Roger to his feet. "Let's go out and sit in the back yard for a while."

Prospero and Roger went out the back door into a cool night filled with lightning bugs that flashed their tiny pulsing lamps in every corner of the garden. A great willow hung in ghostly silver near the faintly trickling fountain, and Prospero's favorite apple tree stretched one long awkward branch up to touch the eaves of the house. The sharp smell of black dirt mingled with the green smell of wet leaves, and a light milky mist lay on the grass. The two weary but still talkative wizards sat in a pair of fan-backed wicker chairs and pitched pebbles at the drunken satyr in the fountain. They talked about wars, enchantments, and obscure facts until the sky above the forest began to be fringed with pale blue. Eventually they collected enough strength to get up and go inside. Prospero took Roger to one of the many spare bedrooms, where the two of them shook out a set of slightly musty sheets and made up the canopied oak bed. On the way back to his room, guttering candle in hand, Prospero noticed that the great ruby-paned iron lamp that hung at the head of the stairs was flickering and laboring as if it had been thrust into a musty cave or a long unopened room. He cast a sharp look down the dark stairs and stood dead still, listening. Crickets and frogs, and far off a restless dog. The light began to burn more brightly, so he blew out his candle and went to bed.

TWO

When Roger Bacon woke up the next morning or, rather, the next noon, he felt something more than the usual muggy heat of August days in the South Kingdom. He felt tension in the air, a tension almost audible, the humming of a high-pitched string. He was inclined to blame this feeling on his own nervous nature, so he took a leisurely bath and started down the hall toward the staircase. Prospero's door was open, but he was not in bed. There was no sound downstairs. Roger tiptoed quietly down the steps, went to the living room, and took a square-headed iron mace down from its hook on the wall. But when he stepped into the hallway, there was Prospero, standing at the front door, holding the linen curtain aside and peering out of the small square window. Without turning, Prospero spoke:

"Put that silly weapon away and go to the kitchen.

There's some bread and marmalade, and I've made some coffee. And we're surrounded."

Roger dropped the mace, which just missed his toe as it fell.

"Surrounded? By whom?"

"By whomever or whatever our friend with the book has decided to send against us. Look."

Roger pressed his face against the small square window. Across the road, under a tall thorn hedge, stood three gray figures.

Roger laughed. "Surrounded? By those three?"

"Oh, there are more. There are at least ten more in the forest to the east of us, and I think there are some waiting up the road, toward Brakespeare. Anyway, numbers don't mean anything. Those things are the agents and the work of a man who probably has more power than we have. He is learning how to use that book, and when he has enough strength— or thinks he has—they will close in."

Roger pounded the door in frustration. "Then why are we having breakfast? Are we going to die gracefully at the table, like gentlemen? Why don't you try something? Between the two of us, we ought to be able to send them back to what's-his-name with their blasted gray robes on fire."

"And what if we can't? Then he'll know what he can do. Right now I don't think he's sure. He wouldn't have sent them if he didn't think that I am some kind of threat to him, although right now I would love to know just *how* I could disturb him." Prospero glanced out the window again and continued. "Even if we do drive them off, we still have him to deal with. I will bet you, Roger, that those things can't do anything until nightfall. So there is certainly time for breakfast."

Roger kicked the iron mace into the corner and followed Prospero to the kitchen, where they ate a big breakfast of ham, scrambled eggs, bread, and quince marmalade. Prospero seemed amused by Roger's nervousness, and this made the latter more and more cranky.

"Now," said Prospero, pushing back his chair, "you are probably wondering what we are going to do. Come on." He got up and went to the cellar door.

"Are we going to hide?" said Roger. "Oh, good! It's been years since I hid in a nice smelly basement."

Prospero was laughing so hard that he had trouble getting down the stairs. He led Roger to a high rampart of cordwood, which he then began to dismantle.

"Oh, I see," said Roger as he helped him. "We're going to burn the house down. *That* ought to throw them off."

When all the wood was cleared away, the two wizards were standing before a black door with a porcelain goose-egg

knob. A yellowed piece of cardboard, held to the door with a red thumbtack, said "Root Cellar."

"Well, I haven't been in this place for several months," said Prospero. "There's no telling what we'll find." He pushed the door open and a rank sweetish smell of decaying vegetables hit them. In the windowless earth-floored room were shelves into which blackened rutabagas were rotting, Mason jars filled with cloudy green dandelion wine, and bushel baskets of wildly sprouting potatoes. Here and there the walls were blotched with white and green fungus, and in a corner, cheesy green-spotted toadstools were squatting. Prospero calmly began to take the jars off the shelves that lined the short wall opposite the door. Then he started to lift the shelves from their curlicued iron brackets. Roger was watching him now with delight, for under the dirt and vegetable growth on the wall was the outline of a small arched door.

"Prospero! You never told me about this!"

"I always meant to, but it never seemed all that important. I began to build it quite a few years ago, but I ran into a little trouble. You'll see what I mean. The door, at any rate, is a success. It responds to one of the oldest door spells in the world."

He placed his hands on the door and whispered a few raspy words that sounded like Arabic—actually, they were corrupt Coptic. The door swung inward with a loud screech, and Prospero, ducking his head, stepped inside and motioned for Roger to follow him. A low-ceilinged dirt tunnel with basalt slabs for steps went spiraling down to a smooth stone floor. At the bottom of the stairs, Roger looked at the long vaulted tunnel before him.

"I knew it," he said. "Gothic arches and little carved monster heads. You would."

33

"Of course," said Prospero, picking up a small tin lantern that hung near the stairs. "Notice the fan vaulting and follow me."

They walked through a tunnel that sloped gently down and took one sharp right-angle turn. Suddenly the tunnel opened into a natural cave, a domed, stalactite-dripping room with a dark cold stream flowing through it.

"Here," said Prospero, "is our problem. I ran into this and had to stop. There's no stone beyond this point, and the earth behind that wall is very mushy. But the tunnel that the stream flows through rises four feet above the level of the water."

Roger was getting nervous again. "Are we going to crawl through the water? Do you know where the stream goes?"

Prospero smiled. "I have it on the authority of a talking fish that this stream runs underground for ten miles and then empties into a small lake in the realm of our old friend, King Gorm. You remember him. Well, I think he has a library like the one in Roundcourt, though not so complete. I've never seen it, but it ought to have a copy of the Register, and I want to look up the crest on that bookplate. It's a start, anyway, and there's a possibility that the owner of such an ugly device might have gotten the book back. And I want to know more about that kindly old fisherman who suddenly volunteers to drown the book for the monk. If the lake isn't stocked with gray ghastlies, we may find something interesting." He looked at Roger, who was still scowling at him. "Oh yes—no, we're not going to crawl. Come upstairs."

Back in the living room, Prospero went to the mantelpiece and took down a small, very accurate-looking ship model. "This," he said, "is what we are going in: the British man-of-war *Actaeon,* which ran—will run—aground on a sand bar during the siege of Charleston in 1776. Do you know, by the way, that Lord Nelson was hit in the head with a cannon ball at the Battle of the Nile? You pick up the damnedest things from that mirror."

Roger looked pained. "I think," he said, "that I'll go get a glass of hard cider."

Upstairs, later, Roger was in Prospero's room helping him pack into a green plush carpetbag such essentials as tarot cards, extra tobacco, and pocket magic books. The magic mirror, after plaguing the two men with questions, was finally beginning to understand what was going on.

"You mean," it said with a scarcely suppressed giggle, "that you're going to make yourselves . . . *smaller?*"

"Yes," said Prospero, blushing. "What of it?"

The mirror broke into hysterical cackles and began to chant in a falsetto voice:

> *"Magic words of poof, poof, piffles,*
> *Make me just as small as Sniffles!*
> *Woo, hoo, hoo, hee, hee, hee!"*

"I'll wager," said Prospero, "that I have the only mirror that wallows in the trash of future centuries."

Roger was nervously opening and shutting the casement window. "I'm worried," he said. "What do you suppose he'll do when he finds we've gone? Will he destroy your house or go down the road and attack the village?"

"I think he will try to find us. He hasn't reached his full strength yet by any means—that is, if the book is as evil as I think it is—and I don't think he'll waste his powers destroying a village or a house out of anger. It has occurred to me that he may not be able to injure my house anyway. The

35

hearthstone was laid by Michael Scott, my teacher, and it has many powerful spells on it. He built a good deal of the house, too, and there are still things about it I don't understand. Why, there's a cupboard that—oh, the devil! Some other time. I guess I've got everything. Good-by, mirror. I trust you can entertain yourself while we're gone."

"I should hope so. I think I'll scare the wits out of the cleaning lady when she comes. I have a very nice scream."

A little later, downstairs, Prospero wrote a note in black crayon and left it on the kitchen table under a bust of the Emperor Pupienus.

Dear Mrs. Durfey,
Will be gone for an indefinite period. Pay no attention to the mirror if it acts up, and in any case you know where the harp case is. You can slip it over him when he's not looking. Don't forget to water the trailing arbutus and the creeping Charlie. Change the water in the large onyx water clock; the other one takes care of itself. Help yourself to the cheese and anything else. The Cheshire gets dry and crusty if you don't eat it. With luck, I should be back for the big Christmas party. Say hello to His Lordship the Mayor for me.
Prospero
P.S. Unexplained noises are best left unexplained.

He looked around the house sadly. "I do hate to leave. Oh, well. Are the windows closed, Roger? Grab your bag and let's get going."

Soon the secret door had closed behind the two wizards and they had placed the boat in the black water, where it rocked gently, moored by a pair of wispy cords. The ship was close to the low bank, and a rope ladder hung down from the muddy edge to the portside rail. Roger Bacon and Prospero stood looking doubtfully at the tiny craft.

"Well," said Roger, "I don't suppose we can put it off."

"No," said Prospero, "I don't suppose we can."

He thumbed a small book, which looked like a pocket dictionary, until he found the page he wanted.

"All together now:

> *Shrivel, shrink, squinch, and squibble*
> *Dwindle, dwilp, melt, and dribble*
> *ZALAMEA ALCAZAR!"*

Roger and Prospero shrank and shrank, until they looked like two odd chess pieces standing by the brown sloping sides of the boat. They made faces at each other, laughed a little, and then climbed aboard.

Inside the low, echoing wet-dirt tunnel, the noise of the rushing water was weirdly magnified and distorted into a hollow tinny roar. A shout or a handclap came whanging back at you immediately from a low curving roof. Prospero and Roger, sliding farther and farther into this claustrophobic gloom, stood on the high ornamented poop of their absurd ship and watched the shrinking half moon of light cast by the lantern they had left on the floor of the cave. Two tiny alcohol-burning stern lamps cast a flickering moth-light on the wizards, who now turned to the task of keeping up their spirits until the *Actaeon* sailed out into the sunny lake.

The ship itself was entertaining, because it was so incredibly detailed: There were gleaming rows of brass cannon, nickel-plated swinging lanterns that worked, and, in the captain's cabin, rows of books, real books, mostly on nautical subjects. Even the purple liquid in the little flattened decanter turned out to be wine. Though they were, if anything, too small for the ship, the wizards still thought of it as tiny, and were endlessly fascinated by the discovery of new details—a cupboard that opened on scrolled brass hinges, a box within the cupboard that held delicate jade-and-ivory chessmen. The wheel, of course, worked, and Prospero had roped it down so that the ship would follow the straight flow of the current. Though all the lamps, lanterns, and candles on board were lit, the sides of the cave could not be seen, and periodic flashes of magic lightning were needed to assure them that the little bobbing toy was still in the middle of the stream.

As the *Actaeon* sailed on into the noisy darkness, Prospero and Roger heard faintly disquieting sounds: the *plip!* that might be a clot of earth falling from the ceiling into the water, the *splop!* that probably was a small water animal sliding off some unseen shore into the stream. And there was another sound, one which was harder to single out from the others and define: It was only a little different from the normal rushing-water sound, yet it *was* there—a hissing and foaming that was getting more and more distinct. At first Prospero thought "Rapids!" and shivered. But it was the sound of water flowing *through* something, not over it. He got up from the powder keg on which he had been sitting and motioned to Roger, who was up on the quarterdeck, trying to compute the speed of the ship. Together they went to the forecastle and stood peering into the blackness ahead. The little swinging lamps that hung near them were not much help, so Prospero and Roger struck their staffs together —a bright red light, dripping like a fireworks flare, hung around them for a few minutes, and by that garish light they saw a mesh of some kind strung across their path. It was held by a rigid black square frame that was awkwardly jammed into the tunnel's rough walls at a point where the opening was lower and narrower than usual.

Prospero and Roger struggled with the capstan, but the anchor was either decorative or stuck. The ship drifted on, yawing a little in the current, until it bumped—more gently than Prospero had hoped—against the strange wall. Prospero set off another flare and suddenly realized what the obstruction was: It was a window screen. *His* window screen. He saw the place where he had scratched with a nail "Bedroom SE Corner," and he remembered the theft, the broken cellar window of three years before. Roger stared at him with understanding and fear.

The ship bumped against the screen, and the water shed through a thousand tiny openings. As Prospero's eyes got used to the dark, he saw that there was a little ledge nearby on one side of the tunnel. And behind it was the deep blackness of a cave. Now from the cave came a scrabbling, grunting, clumping sound, and out of the ragged opening crawled a hairy, angular shape. Two red eyes glowed in the darkness. Prospero could have lit the tunnel for a better look, but the magic was not endless, and anyway he knew what the thing was. So did Roger, who gripped his own staff tightly.

And now a sneering gritty voice:

"Well, well. I hear this noise, so I says to myself—fresh fish! But it ain't, it's a couple of little men in a toy boat!"

Prospero leaned over the side and shouted: "We are wizards, troll! And if you don't let us through this thing we'll turn you into a rock at the bottom of this stinking, filthy, sloppy stream!"

The troll snickered, a nasal snortling sound. "If you're wizards, you can blast your own hole in my screen, can't you? But you ain't done it because you *can't*. So I think I'll have some nice stewed wizard, or wizard dumplings, or"— here he held up the tiny white bones of some animal and rattled them—"wizard gizzard!"

"Troll," said Prospero quietly, with both hands on the rail, "I am going to turn you into lead. A few centuries from now someone will find you and use you for a lawn ornament!"

"Oh, shut up, you mouthy little bug!" said the troll. "I'm going to watch you a few minutes, and then—" He twisted his hands as if he was wringing out a cloth.

Prospero closed his eyes and tried to think. He had been reading about trolls the night Roger came, but now he could think of nothing that would help him. He couldn't even grapple physically with the troll, since the spell that made the two men smaller lasted till sunset, which was at 8 P.M. that day. His watch said five. Picking up his staff and throwing it down in anger, he turned to Roger, but Roger was gone.

"All right," said the troll, lowering his webby feet into the water, "you two ain't no fun no more. You'll probably taste like water rats, but . . ."

A hatch clattered behind Prospero and Roger reappeared, carrying a length of rope from which a four-pronged grappling hook hung. Standing a little back from the rail, Roger whirled the grapnel whistling around his head, and then he let it go. The hook raked the screen but fell into the water, and Roger quickly started to reel it in.

The troll was still sitting on the muddy bank, his feet in the sloshing water.

"This is more like it," he said. He clapped his hands, and when he pulled them apart they went *thock* like suction cups. "Climb to the top and fall over, and then I can rescue you!"

Roger threw the grapnel again, and this time the pronged iron went *chunk!* into the screen—two spurs were wedged tight. Now Roger whipped the rope around the

mainmast and started to pull. Prospero suddenly saw what was going on, and in a second he was pulling too. A large ragged piece of the screen ripped out, crumbling as it fell and spattering the deck with red flakes of rust. The troll stood up and started to stoop forward, but Prospero gathered all his strength and blacked out the tunnel. For several minutes the place was absolutely dark—it was filled with thick, palpable, gross darkness, and while the murk lasted, the little boat slipped through the hole. One scuttering wire scraped the bottom of the hull from one end to the other, and for a sickening instant the boat slowed. But then it bobbed through, wallowed sideways in the current for a bit, and straightened out to steer its course down the middle of the fast-flowing stream. The troll still held his eyes and screeched, for he thought he had been struck blind. Roger and Prospero were far downstream when the lights went on again.

THREE

After more than two hours of uneventful drifting, the
Actaeon rounded a sweeping curve, and Prospero, who was
sitting on one of the bow chasers, saw a blue twilight glimmer ahead. He pointed this out to Roger, who was poking
a straw into the touchhole of the other brass cannon to see
if it really was bored all the way through.

"Oh yes. The lake," said Roger without looking up. He
was determined to be nonchalant until Prospero asked him
one question. "All right," said Prospero, drawing a deep
breath. "How *did* you know the screen was rusted through?"

"A very simple matter, my dear Prospero. You made that
screen twenty years ago. It has been in the tunnel for three
years. So I looked in *Captain Monkhouse's Table of Rust
Rates,* one of the books in the ship's library, and I calculated
the rest with the aid of my little pocket hygrometer."

"Little pocket hygrometer! I don't believe you."

Roger held up a turnip-shaped gold watch on a long twisted chain. The large ticking bulb was covered with glassy warts, crystal-domed dials that told lunar eclipse dates, the rate of rainfall on the third planet out from Alpha Centauri A, and, incidentally, the time.

"I'm sorry I asked," said Prospero, grinning. "Tell me, how far off is sundown?"

Roger squinted at the watch. "Oh, about twenty minutes."

"Hum," said Prospero. "I do hope no one is out fishing on the lake. I'm not sure what I'd do if I saw a wee little ship scooting past my rowboat, but I think I might be tempted to smack it with an oar."

A few minutes later the *Actaeon* floated out onto the windy blue-shadowed water of a little round lake. On the shore were high tossing willow trees and thick clumps of those strange telescoping green reeds that can be pulled apart into sections. In the western sky a tall light-seamed thunderhead was slowly rising to meet two sculptured pink-gray clouds. The *Actaeon*, spinning and at times heeling over dangerously, was swept by the harsh gusts into a squeaking forest of reeds near the shore, where it soon was lodged tight.

Prospero peered through the yellow-banded green columns and listened. From the dark bushes on the shore came voices.

"Of course it's a duck. What else would it be?"

And then the other voice, rumbly and sarcastic:

"Really? How many ducks do you know that spin around and around while they swim?"

"Shut up. You'll scare it away."

Now Prospero and Roger could see two hunched men in the olive light; one of them was quite fat. Probably off-duty soldiers, since they both wore wide-brimmed pot helmets and carried crossbows. "I've always hated duck hunters," whispered Prospero. "I wonder if there's something I can do . . . let's see . . . Oh, good grief! If I had thought of it back there we wouldn't have had any trouble with that troll!" He hit himself on the head with the flat of his hand. "I wonder if I would have thought of it if things had *really* come to a crisis. Oh well . . ."

"What *are* you talking about?" said Roger.

Prospero took off his hat, smoothed down his hair, put the hat back on again, and shook his sleeves back.

"Just watch," he said. "Oh, by the way, how much time do we have now?"

"About three minutes, if your almanac is right."

"Just enough time," said Prospero as he began to make rapid hand passes over the deck. Roger heard him chanting in a low voice, and caught the Celtic word for Greek fire couched between two old Dutch swear words. Suddenly there was a long, loud, ripping crash, as pinpoints of fire shot from the thirty-two cannon of the *Actaeon*. A great bluish cloud rose over the ship and the guns went off again. One hunter jumped up and ran, stumbling through the thorn bushes, screaming "Yaaaaaah! Spirits from the vasty deep!" The other fainted, and when he came to, he saw a pair of bearded men standing over him. Both were wet to the waist, and laughing. The shorter had just crammed a toy boat into his Gladstone bag.

"Could you tell us," said Prospero politely, "which of the absurd, small, foolish countries of the South we are in?" He knew very well where he was, but he wanted to hear the soldier's reply.

The prostrate man, a potbellied sergeant with a President Cleveland mustache, looked offended.

"You're in the Grand Union of the Five Counties. Population 7200. Our motto is 'Si quaeris terram amoenam, circumspice.' That's Latin. We don't think our country is small."

"You can think what you like," said Roger as he helped the man up. "I believe your king is Gorm III, surnamed the Wonderworker."

The sergeant was beginning to recover his stuffy composure, and he would have leveled his crossbow at these two intruders if he had been able to find it. Prospero had thrown it into the middle of the lake.

"Well," hrumphed the sergeant, "you seem to know so much, maybe you can tell me what you're doing here. There's three feet of stinking water in King Gorm's dungeons, and you're going to be sitting in it."

"Oh stop!" said Prospero impatiently. "King Gorm converted his dungeons into handball courts, and he uses his rack to stretch taffy. Now take us to him or I'll make your mustache light up."

The guard looked at Prospero for a minute, and then he shrugged. "Oh well, you live in a poor little country, and nobody cares if people make fun of you. Come on. It's about two miles."

Prospero and Roger, led by the puffing sergeant, followed a sandy path that wound through scratchy thorns and springy green burdock boughs. Soon, after they had crossed an acre of dung-spotted cow pasture, they were walking on one of the main highways of the South Kingdom, the Great South Road. It was one of the works of Godwin I, and it was paved with hexagonal granite blocks, some of which were stamped with the King's arms and the phrase "Good Roads." Every hundred miles or so you would find by the roadside a statue of Godwin, crowned, seated, and with his hands on his knees in the Egyptian manner, resting after his conquests. What conquests were referred to would be hard to say, since Godwin inherited the South Kingdom through a series of dynastic perversions, freaks, and mishaps much too tedious to discuss here.

At any rate, the road took the three men through a small chestnut forest, over rain-grooved stones covered with green spiny pods, and out onto a broad, stubbly, treeless plain. There, far ahead but clearly visible, stood the castle of King Gorm the Wonderworker, a not very invulnerable fortress that just stood, naked, there in the middle of the plain, without protecting wall, barbican, or moat. For years the castle had simply been a tall stone box fringed with battlements, but at the southeast corner Gorm had added a tall fieldstone tower, capped by a paneled ice-cream cone roof. On three levels were long lancet windows with malachite sills, but they were blacked out from the inside by heavy brown curtains. Prospero and Roger knew very well what the tower was for, and they laughed at the sight of it.

Before long the wizards stood outside the mahogany front door of Gorm's castle, and they waited as the sergeant pounded importantly on the varnished dark wood. Very soon there was a screeching of bolts and a clatter of chains, and the door opened. In the light of a torch that he carried himself stood a small, wizened, eagle-beaked man in a black velvet gown. A chain of linked gold medallions hung loosely around his neck.

"There's a couple of old men here that say they're wizards," said the sergeant. "They want to see the King."

"The King," said the old man in an artificially cadenced voice, "is drowned deep in drafts of doom. With thrilling thoughts he is thrust through, pierced with the press of pointed pinions."

"Nahum," said Prospero, "we do not have time for Anglo-Saxon verse. Is he in the tower?"

The old man looked at them both, coughed, and raised his eyebrows. Though he did not drop his manner, he waved them in. "Hither may ye come, by light of draft-blown cressets, and herein may ye find our crownèd King, with weight of statecraft almost bent to earth."

He led the wizards through a long drafty hall lined with shields, axes, and stuffed falcons. At the end of the corridor was an obviously new door, framed by a high lapis lazuli arch. On a ledge overhead was a bas-relief showing the earth supported by two toads; around the globe was a banner that said "MY WORKS PREVAIL." Nahum the seneschal rapped lightly on the paneled door. After about five minutes the door was opened by a vague-looking middle-aged man in a stiff gold brocade robe covered with seed pearls arranged in geometric designs. His moon face was clean shaven, and he wore thick rimless glasses that made his eyes swim like huge protozoa.

Nahum bowed and spoke. "Most intransigent monarch, two wanderers, whose years hang about them like millstones, though their wisdom rattles beads in the nursery of the mind, seek humble access to your cloud-bedizened person."

The wavy eyes grew bigger behind the bottle glass. "Oh, good heavens! It's Prospero and Roger. Come in. Nahum, you should stop studying rhetoric books and go back to Beowulf. I like the alliterative style better."

Nahum bobbed again. "My crest is cropped by croaking cranes. I go to drown in doleful dumps, dead-drunk with drearihead." He turned and left.

Prospero and Roger entered a dark echoing silo that seemed to be full of humming, crackling fireflies. The tower had only one room, and the walls, ringed by galleries at intervals, rose a hundred feet to the conical roof. In the great dark void above the wizards' heads hung tiny galaxies, solar systems, and nebulae. Checkered, spotted, and marbled planets moved around flaring orange suns the size of Ping-pong balls. Multi-ringed Saturns were surrounded by clouds of pinhead moons, and three-tailed comets roared through spinning clusters of stars with a noise like toy locomotives. Gorm was a magician, but an introspective one, a model-railroad hobbyist. Now he stood staring delightedly up at the clicking, clanging, flashing pinball machine he had been working on for forty years.

"We've been having some trouble with Sector 8," he said, waving a wooden pointer. "A couple of planets are doing a horn-pipe, and before long—apocalypse! I think we must blame the terrible black planet Yuggoth, which rolls aimlessly in the stupefying darkness. Ooop! Watch out!"

All three hit the floor as a five-pronged comet, looking like a Chinese kite, came whooshing down at them. It dusted the floor with its tails and roared up again into the sparkling indoor night. Prospero picked himself up. "Gorm, I know you want us to stay for a supernova or something, but we're in a hurry. Do you have the key to the Hall of Records?"

Gorm looked vague. "Key . . . 'there was a door to which I had no key' . . . very fine, Persian decadent writers. Made handsome rugs too, some of them. Oh yes. The curator has one, but visiting hours are from two to two-thirty Monday through Wednesday, and he is not likely to be around. No, I shouldn't think so. But I have a key. Keep it on a chain

around my neck. If he *is* there, show it to him and tell him I sent you. Are you sure you can't stay? One of these galaxies is going to go off in a little bit."

"Thanks," said Prospero, "but we've got to get going. As it is, it'll be midnight when we get there. I wish I could tell you what's going on, but I'm not sure of anything myself."

King Gorm looked at Prospero with a sad smile. "You know, the trouble with you is that you don't have any purpose in your life. Always running in and out."

He reached inside the heavy pearled neckband of his gown and pulled out a long chain, at the end of which hung a snaggle-toothed brass key. He took the key off the chain and handed it to Prospero. "I hope you'll excuse the mess inside the Hall," said Gorm. "I never can get the curator to straighten things up. The last time I was there I found him correcting books to prove that my universe here was the best one ever made. I hit him with a copy of Ptolemy, and he's been testy ever since."

A staticky mechanical voice from high up in the tower burst in: ". . . cool and cloudy this evening with snow in spiral nebulae. Total solar eclipse in galaxies 3, 5, and 6, followed by meteor showers. Observers are advised to take cover. Supernova will obliterate Galaxy 12 later tonight, this being no great loss since it never did work right anyway . . . (click) . . . Thank you."

Prospero and Roger edged toward the door, shouting thanks at King Gorm, who was still squinting up at the ceiling. And then they were gone. Out on the plain, a few minutes later, they stopped and looked back at the castle. The tower roof flipped suddenly up like the lid on a beer stein, and a fizzing skyrocket shot up. When it burst, little

52

green stars spelled out "So Much for Galaxy 12," and pinwheels on parachutes floated down to earth, whistling *Anacreon in Heaven.*

Prospero shook his head. "Well, at least *he's* happy. Come on, it's getting late."

They were back on the South Road, which ran straight for several miles and then dropped into a narrow cleft between two low, crumbling, prehistoric forts made of flat unmortared stones. Occasional lightning flashes lit the spreading western thunderhead, showing fantastic cloudcliffs and tumbling gorges. Dull rumbles in the distance. It was midnight by Roger's watch when they saw a low black shadow in the pines and junipers at the side of the road. A powdery dirt path ridged with tree roots led to the one-story stone building.

The Hall of Records looked like an abandoned cottage: Mossy hatchet-shaped slates scalloped the roof, and one broken windowpane was patched with a waxed vellum sheet from a psalter. The peeling orange door sank into a ground-level sill, and the jawless skull of a groundhog chewed the dirty white lintel. Prospero pulled out the key—it glowed a little in the faint moonlight—and he pushed aside the tin cup that covered the rusty lock. *Crrrrrunk!* and the key went all the way around, but he had to kick the door several times before it scraped in, following a curving groove in the wooden floor.

As Prospero stepped in, his cheek was touched by the rough cold muzzle of a stuffed alligator that hung from the ceiling. He stepped back and turned to Roger.

"You'd better stay outside and watch for the curator—or anyone else who might visit us. This shouldn't take too long, though God knows I've never been inside this place before."

"All right. You've got the copy of the bookplate, and you know the book you want. Good luck." Roger turned and walked down the path to a broad gray stump. He sat down and lit his red clay pipe.

Inside the one-room building irregular piles of books were scattered about in the ashy darkness. Tiny matchbox-sized books stood in tottering spires on broad elephant folios, and three big square ledgers lay chained to a slanted reading desk against the far wall. Prospero was interested in these ledgers. He lit a candle stub and stuck it on the dirty window sill over the desk. When he had brushed a thin coat of dust off the pebbled leather cover of one volume, he saw the words: *Register of All Wizards and Warlocks of the South Kingdom and of the North from the Beginning of the World to the Present Time.* He turned the thick damp-smelling pages of the book, looking for the crest that was on the crumpled sheet in front of him—and there it was. The evil device was carefully drawn in black ink, and below it was an unusually long entry in a thick-lined runic script. But Prospero was looking at the name. He was staring at it because it was a name he knew: MELICHUS.

"He has a new crest," whispered Prospero in the dusty darkness.

He took out his gold-rimmed glasses, put them on, and hunched over the ledger. The greater part of the entry was not very helpful; in fact, Prospero knew more about Melichus' past than the author did. But at the bottom of the page there was a note in a scribbly secretarial hand, probably that of Gorm's curator. The ink was fairly fresh and had blotted on the opposite page.

"I have discovered by divers means that the above M. was in England some LXX yrs. ago, living among fishermen to learn sea-spells. After his return to the S.K. he took up his abode in the village of Briar Hill where he lived a secluded life. About that time the townsfolk began to be visited by the apparitions of their dead relatives and friends. Faces were seen at windows, and shapes were seen in the streets during storms. All suspected M., and he admitted as much to their faces, but their threats were of no avail, till the wife of one D.L. was frightened at noontime by some horrid form, so that she jumped before a cart and horses & was killed. L. gathered a group of men who went one night to the house of M., armed with clubs and scythes. As they were battering on the door, M. escaped by a cellar window, but was seen & a chase ensued. The townsmen followed M. to a small forest some III mi. from the town, where L. wounded him with a bowshot. The wizard entered the forest & was lost in the darkness, but L., who was still angered beyond reason, persuaded his fellows to ring the forest about and guard all the ways of egress. Maddened by him, they set a blaze which well nigh consumed the whole wood, so that the next morning they found within the burnt body of M., wch. they buried in the forest clearing where he fell. The forest has grown back, but not as before, and I myself would not go within it night or day. The townsmen call it the Empty Forest, since animals & birds do not live there. Obiit Melichus Magister A° 697 A.U.C."

Prospero stood over the glimmering yellow page, gripping the book with both hands. A bit of plaster dropped from the ceiling onto the paper, startling him, and he jumped back, looking around wildly. The room was quiet, but overhead he heard hollow tumbling sounds. The thunderhead must be moving in fast now, he thought. A leafy branch swished across a window and an acorn rolled all the way down the roof. Now he could hear the wind hissing in the pines.

Usually Prospero enjoyed storms, but this one, like the storm of the day before, oppressed him in a strange way. He found it was all he could do to go across the room to the doorway, where he stood looking out into the windy tossing night. Big splatting drops were starting to fall, and from where he stood by the sagging orange door he could see Roger hurrying up the path, pulling up his hood to keep off the rain, which now began to sweep by in long gray sheets.

As Prospero stood there waiting for Roger, he began to feel more and more strange. The feeling reminded him of a time when he had been sitting by the fire one night on the verge of a very bad cold. Everything around him—outdoor noises, the normal creakings of the house, the ticking of the clocks—had seemed distant and muted. That was how things seemed now: His face prickled, he felt hot, and it was hard for him to move. Though he had important news for Roger, he did not feel like saying anything.

Roger brushed past him and stopped in the middle of the room. "Well, shut the door." His voice was sharp and almost contemptuous.

Prospero struggled to push and lift the door back into place, and when he had finished, his forehead throbbed and the tipsy orange rectangle seemed blurred. He went to a nearby window and stood looking at the running ice-gray pane. Roger lit a two-socketed candelabrum and set it on a pillar of books in the center of the room. The streaming rain and the reflected candlelight made strange disturbing dancing shapes in the window. Gray figures waving their arms. Without turning, Prospero spoke in a throaty feverish voice. "Roger, I have found something here."

"Have you?" Roger laughed, but it was the wrong kind of laugh and it ended on a barking sound.

Prospero stared harder at the glimmering square that was crawling before his eyes.

"You aren't Roger, are you?"

"No," said the figure behind him. "I am not, though I wear his cloak and carry his staff. A staff which supposedly can only be wielded by the great sorcerer himself. Let us see."

Prospero heard a sharp rap behind him and saw a sickly yellow light dance for a few moments on the dust-webbed walls, like a flare-up from an almost dead fire. The air around him was heaving now. He felt as if he were at the bottom of the sea.

"Not a very good light, perhaps," said the figure. "But soon there will be none at all. Right now Bacon is being led into the forest by two of Gorm's soldiers, who think they are under orders from the King to execute a warlock. I summoned them after I had disarmed your friend. They will probably strike his head off when they find a log they can use for a chopping block."

Now Prospero could not have turned around if he had wanted to. He had to grit his teeth and stare to keep from losing consciousness.

"How could you disarm him?" he said.

"Very easily. I serve someone who has more power than both of you together. My master will spare you if you go home and wait. He will not harm you if you go home and stay there. After his victory you may want to serve him. Do you know what happens to a wizard's staff when the wizard dies?"

Prospero saw the wavering cowled shape reflected in the candlelit pane. It held a long black staff. Suddenly there was a loud crack and the staff bent, twisted, writhed into an ugly bent branch covered with cancerous scabbed growths. The figure cast the shuddering piece of wood to the floor and said quietly:

"He is dead. Go home."

Prospero was alone in the dark room. The rain clattered on the loose slates and went *pock! pock!* at the parchment nailed over the broken pane, until a sudden gust blew the sheet loose and threw a spatter of rain on the floor. He stood there all night, his hands on the window sill. He stared at the lines and scratches in the wood as if he were trying to find a pattern. Someone had scratched the nonsense Latin word *"Necreavit"* into the sash, and he stared at this for some time. A black beetle climbed the speckled pane, and somewhere in the back of the creaking room a fly was buzzing and bumping stupidly against a window. The wet wind, blowing through the broken pane, riffled through a thick book spread open on the floor.

The rain stopped, and the streaked pane grew gradually lighter as an overcast humid day dawned. Prospero straightened and flexed his stiff dirty hands. He picked up his staff and satchel, forcing his eyes away from the stick on the floor, and he wrenched open the door, shut it, locked it, and put the key over the lintel. Prospero looked at the split and crumbling stump where Roger had sat the night before, and he grimaced. Staff in hand, he walked stiffly down the muddy path to the stone-paved highway, where he stood for a minute looking at the still puddles that lay in the cracks and smooth-worn hollows of the road. He set out walking with long strides, and the direction he took was not toward home.

FOUR

Prospero walked quickly along the Great South Road, and as he walked he argued with himself. Sometimes he would stop and wave his staff at some objection he was trying to dismiss, or he would speak aloud phrases like "Of course not!" or "Spared me out of good will, did he?" But after a while he walked more slowly and talked less. When he came to a mossy stone bench that was half sunk into a muddy red clay bank, he sat down on it, put his head in his hands, and cried. After a while he looked up and wiped his eyes with a big linen handkerchief.

"Well," he said, "I can't allow myself to believe that Roger is dead. I think whoever-he-is would have killed me too if he had had the power. He tried before, didn't he? Roger must be alive. But then where is he? At any rate, I have to go on. There's something I've got to find out." He got up and started out again.

The day cleared up as Prospero walked along, and it was a bright hot noon when he came to the place where the Great South Road crosses the Sea Road, which runs from the wellsprings of the Pipestone River to the sea forts on the western coast. At this major crossroads was a gallows tree, a huge oak held together by brass hoops bolted around the pitted and barkless trunk—it had been dead for the last ten years. People told stories about a time, three centuries before, when bodies hung from every limb. That was during the Seven Princes' War, which had left the South Kingdom a smoking land of burned cities, leveled fortresses, and trampled wheat fields. It was the last civil war the South Kingdom ever had, but it was bad enough to bring on the Long Plague, which killed so many that even by the time of this story, the country was still underpopulated.

The tree had not been used much since the Seven Princes' War, and it had not been used at all after the grandfather of the present Duke Anselm abolished the death penalty in his lands. That is why Prospero was shocked and horrified to see a body dangling from one dead limb. He was relieved a minute later, though still puzzled, when he saw that it was a crude straw dummy in a ragged brown robe. A piece of paper was pinned to its chest, and when he got close enough to read it, Prospero was shocked again. The word "Wizard" was written there in the three principal languages of the South, and under it were large ugly runes that not many people knew about. They were used when one magician wanted to destroy another.

Prospero stared at the swinging manikin, and after a

little thought decided to leave it where it was, since he knew that rune-spells were sometimes activated when you tried to burn the effigy. Now, before he set out again, he took out a wrinkled map-book that had main routes marked in red, and spent some time tracing the twistings of the Sea Road with his finger. Briar Hill was still half a day's walk away, and though he was tired from lack of sleep, he knew that he did not dare to try camping overnight on the road. He had felt a foreboding long before he came to the tree, and as he walked on into a smeary crimson sunset, his fear grew. For some time he had been nagged by the maddening feeling that someone was moving in the thickets near the road or waiting just out of sight around a bend. As the last dark fringe of light faded over the long grassy ridges, Prospero stopped at the bottom of a low hill and listened. A little way behind him, started by something, a small stone began to roll, and it rolled until it came to rest at his feet. There was nothing against the pear-green sky at the top of the hill. Prospero looked at the stone curiously and turned to go on.

He had not gone a mile when he saw, off in a clearing beyond some beech trees, the light of a campfire. At least there'll be *someone* to talk to, he thought, and he stepped off the road into the swishing wet grass. But as Prospero got near the fire, he saw that there was no one tending it and that it was burning in a very strange way. The flames moved back and forth as if blown by suddenly shifting breezes. As he watched, the movement became rhythmical. Prospero looked about him with growing fear, and he noticed that there was a little stream running nearby. He was drawn by what he first took to be a reflection of the firelight on the water. But as he knelt by the stream he saw that the faint glow came from *beneath* the surface of the water. There on the bottom, in a speckled green trembling light, was a smooth triangular stone, and on it was painted his face. The moving water was slowly flaking away the paint, or whatever it was, and the face appeared to be slowly decomposing. He saw a thin film, like a piece of dead skin, wriggle off the portrait-mask and float away down the stream. And the face underneath . . . Prospero felt his own hands on his wet cheeks.

Against all his instincts, he plunged his hands into the greasy-feeling, incredibly cold water and picked up the stone. Without looking at it, and holding it at arm's length as if it were a rotten dead bird, he took it to the fire, which was dancing faster now—it was moving to the rhythm of his own heartbeat. He knew the words that must have been said: "When the fire dies, let him die too."

He pulled a burning stick out of the fire and held it to the painted stone as he carefully recited a spell he could just barely remember. When the face on the stone was completely blackened, the thing turned to an awful viscous mush in his hand, like a potato left in a damp dark cellar. With a disgusted shudder and a quick jerk of his left arm, Prospero threw the pulpy thing into the stream, where it hit with a gulping sound. Now the whole stream began to boil, and out of the lurching, hissing water rose a smoke shape with arms. It moved toward Prospero and settled around him in swaying layers of mist. He felt as if his eyes were made of blank white chalk. And the thing was throbbing, to pump the life out of him. Prospero stared with open eyes into that stony nothingness, and he shouted a word that sorcerers can only speak a few times in their lives. The whiteness began to break, and he could see night through the cracking clouds. Now he began to speak like someone reciting a lesson: "Michael Scott is buried in Melrose Abbey. A light burns in his tomb day and night. And it is stronger than your freezing white. Go! In his name, go!"

The mist blew away, and Prospero was standing in a starlit clearing full of the welcome noise of strident crickets. The fire was out, but he stepped on all the embers and made signs in the air over the black sunken heap of sticks. Now he was alone, and he stood panting and sweating as a cool wind smelling of wood smoke blew in his face. With a sudden, stiff, stooping movement, he grabbed his staff and bag and walked back toward the road.

Suddenly he heard a loud noise in the distance, and he was about to get ready for another attack when he recognized the sound. It was a wagon of some kind jolting along the rutty road. Prospero took out his bent and knobby pipe and lit it, and before long a rattling horse-drawn wagon loaded with split logs came around the bend. By the haloed light of two swaying oil lanterns Prospero could see the driver, a big kind-looking man in a fringed green jacket.

"Hello there!" Prospero shouted. "Which way are you going?"

"Briar Hill. I live there. Would you like a ride?"

"I certainly would," said Prospero.

He threw his satchel into the back and climbed up alongside the driver. Before long Prospero was telling stories about the great castle which had stood on the site of Briar Hill, and the driver was nodding and listening appreciatively. The road wound more now and began to climb steep rounded hills covered with shaggy grass and bent old apple trees. After several hours of bumping over this twisting trail, they came to the bottom of one hill that was much higher than the rest. It was surrounded at its base by a very thick, cruel-looking thorn hedge, originally the outer wall of the castle that had stood on the hill until the Seven Princes' War, when it was taken and partially torn down. Many of the houses of Briar Hill were built with stones from this castle, and the sprawling briar tree that gave the town its name still grew in what was once a courtyard. One or two high jagged walls, pierced with cross-shaped loopholes and long narrow windows, still stood in odd places, up against homes or blocking off alleyways. The two openings in the hedge, on the east and west sides of the hill, had once been guarded by bronze doors and low stone watchtowers. But at this time there was only a night watchman, who waved his bull's-eye lantern at the lumber wagon as it went in.

As the wagon bumped and jolted into the moonlit town square, Prospero looked around at the houses, mostly thatched, comfortable-looking places with half-timbered and overhanging second stories. Between two of these he saw the roofless, burned-out shell of a one-story stone cottage. The front wall was covered with complicated hex signs that must have been painted and repainted over the years. Above the door was a Gothic *M* with many lines drawn through it in red paint.

"Well," said the driver, reining in the horses, "here we are. If you want an inn, there's the Gorgon's Head over there."

"Thanks," said Prospero. "I can't tell you how much I appreciated that ride." I can't tell you, he thought, because if I did, you and the other townsfolk would probably escort me to the west gate. Prospero had a rough idea of the popularity of magicians in a town like this. As the wagon rolled away, he stood in the dusty street a minute, wondering whether he ought to go to Melichus' house. Well, maybe in the morning.

He crossed the square to the Gorgon's Head, which was named for something that must have been part of the old castle: a stone monster with bulging eyes and wrinkled protruding tongue. The marvelously ugly head stood in a niche over the inn door, and it was badly copied on a signboard outside. Prospero dearly wanted to reach up with his staff and make the gorgon's tongue go in and out, but he was afraid someone might be watching him, so he went on inside and arranged for a room. When the landlord brought out the guestbook, Prospero thought for a full minute before signing. The man looked at him strangely.

"Oh, come now," he said. "It can't take that long to think of your name."

"Hm? Oh no," said Prospero. "I was just noticing that rusty old broadsword over the mantel. I'll bet there's a story behind that."

There certainly was, and a very tedious one, but by the time the landlord had finished telling it, Prospero had thought of a name he might use. He didn't know for sure if the people here had heard of him, but a name like Prospero was not common and it was the kind a magician might have. He signed the guest book as Nicholas Archer of Brakespeare (Brakespeare was the name of the village near Prospero's home), adding his usual loop-and-squiggle device under the name, in case Roger should come this way looking for him.

Though he was tired, Prospero played several games of tarot and old-man's-hatchet with the other guests in the common room, and after a supper of crusty veal pie and brown beer, he went up the gritty stone stairs to his bedchamber. It was the end of August but the night was chilly, so a small fire had been built in the little fireplace, which was carved to look like a gaping toothy mouth. Prospero stood by the window and looked across the square at the tumbled ruins of Melichus' cottage. He knew what he had to do the next day and he did not like it at all.

But he shrugged and went to his satchel, and from it he took his large manuscript magic book and a mahogany tobacco box. The inn provided a rack of fresh clay pipes; Prospero took one, lit it, and sat down in an ugly but comfortable wooden chair near the fireplace. Villagers then did not usually read in the bedrooms of inns, if they read at all, so there was no lamp other than a single bedside candle in a brass holder. But Prospero had come prepared: He reached into the tobacco box, and out of the shaggy brown strands he pulled a small silver snuffbox. He set it on the floor beside him and rapped it twice with his ring finger. There was a ping, the box popped open, and out of it grew what looked like a copper sunflower stalk, which sprouted to the height of four feet. The stalk burst into bloom, and a hissing gaseous flower started to dance over Prospero's head, casting a bright yellow light around the man and his chair. He had taken the precaution of closing the inside shutters of the only window, and his staff, though it leaned lightly on the door, was capable of keeping out anyone who did not want to smash his way in with an ax.

Prospero leafed through the book till he came to a section with the black-letter heading "Necromancy." These pages did not have the grease stains and bottle marks that the others did, because Prospero had never had to use this section of his book. Years before, many years before,

68

he had copied down what Michael Scott had taught him. Now, like a novice, he pored over pentagrams and circles, and his long tobacco-stained forefinger ran back and forth over strange curlicued words and long dark-sounding chants. He read for about an hour, and then, though he was trying to stay awake, he slumped farther and farther forward. The pipe slipped out of his left hand and broke with a little pop on the hearthstone, scattering dots of red ash that soon went out. The book slid off his knees onto the floor, and the light-bloom, now that Prospero did not need it, went out and shrank on withering stalk into its box.

Prospero dreamed at first that he was home, letting himself in the back door on a bright moonlit night. The gargoyles over the back porch shone gray, and one reached down to touch his hat as he went in. He went up the stairs to his bed. But the door of his bedroom kept opening and he had to get up to shut it over and over again. Then a storm arose outside and white things shrieked past the window, scratching at the pane. The door of his room opened again slowly, and the front door flew in with a crash that broke the glass window. Prospero got halfway down the stairs, and from there he saw a man in the doorway. The man's shadow stretched across the room, and he was beckoning to Prospero. Then Prospero found himself running through a forest at night, and behind him floated large silent owls. They drifted and hung like paper lanterns, and their impossibly big eyes glowed yellow. When one owl scraped him he shuddered violently, for it felt like a hollow parchment husk. All of Prospero's fear of dry insect shells, crackling, peeling, dusty things with skeletal limbs, choked him and made him thrash around in the chair until he woke up.

Immediately he sat up straight and looked around the dark room. Nothing was wrong. He shook the ashes off his lap and went to the window to open the heavy shutters and let in the chilly night. Across the empty square the stretched mask of an orange-brown moon was setting behind the wreckage of Melichus' house. The briar tree hissed and tossed a little and then was quiet. Prospero left the window and checked the staff, which was still propped against the door. He went to the plain oak bed, turned back the sheets that smelled a little of cedar nuts, and stretched out under the blankets till his feet touched the solid footboard. Prospero slept quietly till morning, dreaming only, as far as he could remember, of floating over housetops in a balloon. He would reach down and spin the weathercocks with his hand.

FIVE

When Prospero awoke the next morning, he stared for a long time at the blinding white clouds that lay along the broken line of gabled rooftops. After a few minutes his eyes began to hurt, so he rolled over and stared at the white blotches that danced in the black mouth of the stupidly ferocious gargoyle fireplace. He feared the day's work, and he wanted (half-consciously) to keep his mind unfocused. But as soon as he was aware of what he was doing, he shook his head, shuddered, jumped out of bed, and began mechanically gathering up his belongings, as if he were collecting firewood.

After he had stuffed books, snuffbox, and tobacco box into his green bag, Prospero looked quickly around the homely little room and took his staff away from the door

As he grasped the heavy stick, the knuckles of his right hand rested momentarily against the thick wooden door, and he had an odd sensation in that instant. It seemed that the wood suddenly *gave* under his hand, as if some pressure from outside had suddenly been removed. Prospero stood there for a few seconds, and then he pulled the door inward so violently that it slammed against the whitewashed stone wall. No one was in the hall, which was still dark, though it was morning outside. A couple of burned-out candle ends dripped wax beards from their sconces.

He went back into the room and lit the bedside candle, which he held up close to the outer face of the door. The wood was crisscrossed over and over with long scratches: some of them were needle scrapes, others were wide and deep, and one ended in a ragged gouge that must have gone halfway through the door. Prospero dropped his candle. When he could think clearly again he began to wonder why the thing hadn't climbed in through the window. The shutters had been open most of the night.

He turned and went back into the room. The window sill was the answer to his question: Some superstitious (or prudent) traveler, days or weeks ago, had drawn a powerful hex sign on the stone sill in rain-blurred yellow chalk. Prospero thanked him, whoever he was, and sat down on the bed.

"I wonder if the landlord was disturbed by the thing?" he said to himself out loud.

This question in its turn was answered by the look on the landlord's face when Prospero went downstairs to pay the bill.

"Keep your witch's money," said the old man, staring

hatefully at him. "And take your magic out of this inn and out of this town. Do I look tired? Well, I've been up all night praying. I don't know what you brought in here last night, but I hope the other guests didn't hear it or *smell* it, the way I did. I'd call the watch and have you put in prison till we could try you and burn you, but they say you can come back after you're dead. The other one did."

Prospero would have explained, but he knew that the response would be another tirade. So he took three gold coins out of his pocket and flipped them casually over his shoulder. They shot the length of the room and were imbedded deep in the limestone mantel of the fireplace, where they are to this day. On his way out, for good measure, he crossed the eyes of the stone gorgon.

As he walked across the square, Prospero thought of his planned investigation of the ruined cottage. That would have to be left to Roger if he came this way, assuming he was alive, and Prospero *was* assuming that his best friend was still alive.

It did not take Prospero long to get to the west gate of the town. But once he was outside the thick spiny hedge, he realized that he didn't have the faintest idea of which way to go. He hardly expected signs, but on the other hand, what was he going to do? Two farmers stood by the city gate, arguing about seed prices. He walked up to them, took off his hat, and bowed.

"Excuse me, but I am traveling north on foot, and I want to avoid going through the forest you people talk about here. The inn was full of terrible stories about it."

One farmer turned and gave him an odd look. "I'm surprised they'd talk about it at all. But if you want to know where it is, so that you can avoid it, I'll tell you. Straight along that dirt road about five miles. If you want to be sure just step off the road and stand inside the forest a bit. Then get out of it and go on. You're safe during the day, as long as you don't go too far in. You'll know when you're in it." He gave Prospero another suspicious look and turned away.

The black mucky road ran straight down the western face of Briar Hill and into a green shadowy cleft. It cut between two banks of shelving mossy sandstone for about three of the five miles Prospero followed it, and then it became a weedy ditch about three feet wide that wound through scratchy bushes and large sprouting ferns with scrolled green fronds. After that, the road stopped—no longer a road, just a wide clearing, flat as a lake and covered with hairy, tangled, yellow grass that lay close to the ground. And on the other side, the forest.

It did not look haunted, especially at noon, this crowded, textured, interwoven wood. Prospero saw every shade of green, from light, bleached, papery, yellow-green to a dark, wet, inky green that was almost black. Willows, poplars, maples, oaks, and stubby kinked mulberry trees. As he crossed the little clearing, he noticed that the wood—at least the part of it that he saw—was surrounded by a loose fence of closely planted wooden poles tipped with spear blades and linked by three tiers of reddish iron chains. Nothing that a man might not break down in a few minutes, but it could keep something in. The gate was more impressive: two heavy round stone pillars, and between them a single spike-topped door of thick pine boards banded with iron. Again, like the fence, this barrier was merely symbolic, since it was fastened by an unlocked metal latch that could be lifted easily. Atop the wide pillars

were two rain-eaten stone statues. The one on the left was a cowled monk who stood facing into the forest with upraised arms; the other statue, a naked, scrawny, kneeling shape, looked out toward the glade, but his hands covered his face. Prospero looked once around him, shifted the heavy bag to his left hand, and lifted the curved latch. The door swung inward very easily, and without noise. When he turned to push it shut behind him, he looked up at the protesting stone monk. The lower half of the face was broken away, leaving in the hollow of the cowl a look of blank gap-mouthed fear.

Once he was actually inside the forest and the oiled gate was shut behind him, Prospero knew what was wrong. There are times when you feel that you hear doors slamming in the distance, voices calling your name; you see blurred things, far away or very close up, that look like people until you focus on them. That was the trouble. The whole place seemed slightly out of focus, very slightly off. If was as if you were half asleep. There was a buzzing in Prospero's ears, and he had to stare at a tree for several seconds before it looked like a tree and not a leaning furry shadow. He felt very nervous, drowsily nervous, with prickling dark borders on his sight. A glass bell was ringing somewhere deep, deep in the forest. An icy green glass bell ridged with frost, trembling on a green willow branch.

Prospero shook his head to clear it of this image. The light on the forest floor, even at noon, was dim, with little wavering circles in clusters here and there. The circles moved back and forth in a way that Prospero did not like; the branches shifted and did strange things just out of his line of vision. After a few minutes, some of the strangeness went away, but the queasy feeling of distortion was still there. He picked a narrow strip of crushed grass and followed it into the close-crowding trees.

As he walked along, Prospero noticed more things that he did not like: Clumps of mangy and wormholed ivy covered what looked like stumps from the fire. But when he tried to scrape the vines away with his staff, the whole tangled mass fell into the ground with a faint plop. There was never any stump, only a damp hole smelling sickly of rotted plants. And what the Register of Wizards revealed was true. This was the Empty Forest. Once or twice Prospero stopped at a tree to look at some small speckled bug stuck in a crevice of bark. When it didn't move, he touched it lightly with his finger. The dead shell flicked away to the ground. And once he thought he saw the amber eyes of a small animal staring at him out of a hollow in the side of an old broken tree. When he went up close to look in at the unwavering stare, he closed his eyes and turned away. The small animal, whatever it was, stood on its hind legs, hunched, mummified, long dead. Eyes that should have rotted had by some awful magic grown hard, like cloudy yellow marbles, and the matted hair was shrunken on the bones.

Prospero walked on into the musty leaf-green light that grew deeper and darker as he went farther in. The trees were very large for a second growth, even a fifty-year-old second growth, and some looked much older than they possibly could have been. Had the whole forest really burned down? It would have taken many years for those thick pebbled humps to grow on the wide, splitting trunks. A very strange place. Then, as he was trudging along through wet clotted leaves, staring at the shelf growths that sometimes laddered the whole north side of a tree, he looked up and found that he was at the edge of another clearing.

It was a wide sunny circle of grass, and in the middle something white and hard caught the afternoon light. Prospero walked out to where the white shape was, and found that he was standing over a long flat stone, a grave marker covered with square chiseled letters in ragged rows. Some of the letters were filled with dirt, though the slab itself was amazingly clean—no bird droppings, no leaf stains or weather streaks. What the inscription said was this:

> Under this stone we have placed the burnt body of Melichus the sorcerer. He did great wrong. May his soul lie here under this stone with his body and trouble us not.

"That is a terrible curse," said Prospero, looking at the quiet branches all around him. "I hope it did not come true, for his sake."

Now he had to wait for dark. All the long afternoon Prospero sat there by the stone, listening in vain for some bird, some squirrel, some fat hovering bumblebee. He did not hear anything but the uneasy leaf rustling that started suddenly and built to a nervous thrashing, as though someone took a bough in his hand and shook it. Then quiet again. And he knew that, when darkness finally came, he would not hear crickets. Out in this central circle the queer vagueness of the forest was not so strong, but when Prospero looked for very long into the confusing crisscross of branches, he found that he had to look away, at the blank blue sky or at the bleached grass, or at the familiar green bag that lay beside him.

Night came at last, chilly and damp, but no dew beaded on the flat face of the stone. When the rough-edged half moon began to climb to the center of the little circle of sky, Prospero got up and opened his bag. The copper hinges squeaked, and he jumped back as if he had been shocked. He tried to laugh at his nervousness, but his own dry chuckle only made him feel more strange. He walked back and forth a few times and wiped his hands on his dusty robe, and then he went back to the bag. He took out a pair of brown beeswax candles and lit them, placing them a few feet apart on the carved stone. Between these he opened his large book to the place he had marked the night before. Then he went to the bag again and took out a square glass jar full of saffron-colored chalk powder. Going back to the book occasionally to check the words, he sprinkled the chalk in two concentric circles around himself and the stone, all the while whispering verses. Sometimes he would speak a word aloud, and then stop to listen before going on. In the space between the two circles, with the same yellow powder, he made signs: Hebrew letters, zodiac symbols, old complicated figures that every magician knew. One wide empty space was left, and in it he slowly wrote "Melichus." First he traced the letters in the dirt with his finger, then he poured in chalk. He got up, took a compass from his pocket, and sprinkled water from a metal jar to the north, the south, the east, the west.

Now he was kneeling over the book again, and he read the same passage aloud three times, each time in a louder voice. Finally he stood up and took his staff in his hand. He tapped the name "Melichus" three times and spoke in a firm voice.

"Melichus, by the power of this circle, and the water I have thrown to the four points, and the words I have spoken, I command you to rise before me. Come forth, you that are dead."

Silence in the moonlit circle, and the two candle flames burned straight up. Prospero waited, but all he heard was a creaking branch. He spoke the same formula again, and again there was nothing. The moon passed slowly out of the circle overhead, and the candles spread into brown maps on the cold stone. Prospero pulled his bag toward him and put the book and bottles in it. The clink of jostling bottles made him laugh a little. Here he was in the night with his absurd fat satchel, stealthily conjuring over an empty tomb. He laughed till the nervousness was gone, and then he stirred around the things in his bag till some of the softer items were on the outside. It wasn't a very good pillow, but he slept. His body was just inside the circle.

When he awoke, it was still night, and as he lay there half asleep he began to notice the swaying of the branches. They ought not to move that way, was all he could think. The forms they were tracing bothered him so much that he sat up on his elbows. He turned his head slightly and saw that something in tattered moon-gray was crawling out of the dark grass at the edge of the wood. A man on all fours, making no sound as he scrambled over the dry grass. Prospero closed his eyes and said over and over to himself, "It cannot come into the circle. It cannot . . . ."

The man stopped at the edge of the chalk line, beside Prospero's head. And when he spoke he had the voice of a boy, panting and wincing in pain.

"I am under that stone. I was his servant. They killed me. Let me go."

Prospero, frightened, lying there staring at a sky containing only one or two weak stars, spoke.

"I did not call you. But if I can set you free, I will."

The boy spoke again. His wet lips were almost touching Prospero's ear. "Go north and kill him. Go north." His voice had an awful rising wailing sound.

Prospero clenched his hands and sat up, looking away from the thing that crouched or floated near him. Now he put his hands to his face and tried to think, and finally he spoke the words he had to speak, one at a time in a shaking voice. He turned his head slowly and looked at the shape, which now began to melt into the hard ground like a spreading lump of gray dirty snow.

But nothing evil left the forest. Prospero stared at the ring of trees and realized that he could *feel* their limbs growing tense. He shook his head to get rid of the pulsing fuzziness in his eyes. Had he said the right words? He sat up straighter, and then bent down over the stone, trying to read the letters by the starlight. For some reason he began to trace the letters with his finger tip, trying to imagine how they looked, and how the wavering lines of square deep-cut symbols ran.

"I thought so!" he said out loud, and he pounded on the stone until his hand was sore. Now he knew the reason for those ragged rows. The rise and fall of the letters, the extra spurs and flourishes the carver had put in, had knit together a curse too strong to be undone by a few mumbled words. Prospero, lying full length on the stone, painfully bent his head backward and looked at the dark sky.

"I wonder what I have done," he said. "I wonder what I have done."

The answer came. As he watched, something like a cloud, but too low for a cloud, moved over the circle of sky. Now even the light of those distant stars was going. It felt as though someone were sliding the lid onto a vault, and Prospero could almost hear stone grinding and sliding overhead. Now it was really dark, a shut-in, musty-closet dark. He felt that if he reached out he would touch hanging cloth, old clothes that he did not want near him. Choking, blinding, afraid even to take a deep breath for fear of what he might draw into his lungs, Prospero started to stumble out of the circle, moving his hands in front of him. He felt nothing there, but he sensed something slipping past his arm and trailing down his finger tips. Now he started to run, and his head hit against a tree trunk with a sickening jolt. He turned, and his left cheek was scratched all the way across by what might have been a branch.

Prospero came to a shuffling stop in the leaves that smelled more strongly than ever of black-green rot. Hanging at his belt was a small quartz globe with a brass rod running through it. He unhooked it and held it up, rubbing it. For years he had used this globe; he had used it on the darkest caves under mountains, and it had always sent out a bright orange light that made fire shadows on the rough stone walls. Now it glowed a foggy green, giving Prospero a thin misty halo to walk in. He saw that he was in the middle of several tall dark trunks, and that the clearing was out of sight, although it might be only a few yards away. What he wanted was the path that led back to the gate. Of course, the path was not there, so he started to walk through the trees, holding the weak lamp in front of him. A vine swished down from a tree, and Prospero reached up to fend it off. His hand closed on sticky, slippery rope, and he pushed the thing away.

Suddenly he saw the path. It might not have been the same one, but anyway it was there, and Prospero took it. The hooked branches pulled back as he walked along in the black silence. No noise now but his soft footsteps on the flattened grass. It seemed to be the same path; at least he thought he recognized a little black bush that grew almost across it. As he approached the bush, it slumped across his way with a rustle and what sounded like a little cry. He stopped and prodded it with his toe—it squealed and ran away. And then there was a hand on his arm.

A voice breathed in Prospero's ear with a wet-leaf smell, and what that voice said, Prospero has never told anyone. He turned, and he grasped an arm, but his hand sank into mud—mud with a center like bone. Frantically Prospero jerked his hand away, and with his other hand he shoved the ball of quartz at this breathing, man-sized form. The globe burst with a flash of chilly lightning. Prospero closed his eyes tight and began shoving mechanically at what he could no longer feel. The smell was gone, and Prospero opened his eyes to find that the forest around him was full of fireflies, the last pale magic of the vanished globe. He could see to get out, but he would have to run to make it, because the little dots of light were already going out.

He ran along the path, trying not to look at the things that were going on around him, and as the last fireflies went out, he reached the gate. Outside the fence the clearing lay in calm starlight. His hand was on the latch when he heard another voice—not the whispering leaf voice but a little girl's weak cry.

"Help me! I can't get out!"

He turned and ran to where he saw a small white blur under a willow tree. But when he clasped the child to him, her head crunched under his hand and the whole body turned to crackling fluttery paper. In the air someone was laughing, and the laughter was more horrible because it was a child's—wet, gulping, and somehow harsh. It did not take long for Prospero to reach the gate again, and this time he slammed the gate open with both hands so hard that it rebounded from the stone post. He caught it from the outside, pulled the iron ring, and the latch hooked.

All the rest of the night Prospero walked up and down in the clearing, watching the forest. It was like something seen through glass, engraved and still, like frost-plants on a windowpane. As soon as it was light he got up and walked back to town. He did not care about the townspeople's hatred now. Outside the city wall was a blacksmith's shop, and Prospero walked up to it calmly, like an old customer. The blacksmith looked up in fear.

"Give me a hammer and a chisel," said Prospero, "or I'll tie all your horseshoes in bowknots."

The man gave him the tools. Prospero went back to the forest and kicked open the gate. He marched straight to the clearing, where he found his hat, bag, and staff untouched in the scuffed yellow circle. With the chisel he hacked away enough of the lettering to undo the awful curse that some local magician had made with rising and falling rows of letters. But even though he had—he hoped—wiped out the curse, he did not want to stay in this place, and in a little while he was on a north-running road—after he had returned his tools to the startled blacksmith.

SIX

Prospero had been walking for several hours on a road that was little more than a pair of yellow ruts, overgrown with bunch grass and goldenrod, that wound between high weedy banks from whose crumbling sides twisted roots stuck out, groping at nothing. Now, as the red flattened sun sank into a wide bar of blue-black cloud and the oak trees atop the banks began to darken with twilight, he started to wonder how far away the next village was. The shadowy banks drew closer together now, and he walked on through overhanging leafy arches, looking for a signpost of some kind. It was full dark night, moonless and starless, when Prospero stopped at the top of a small hill to examine something planted a little way off the roadside. He swished away some tall wet grass and straggly bushes with his staff, until he could get to the object that had attracted his attention, and when he struck a match its faint sulphurous light showed a worm-eaten gray post to which a sign was nailed. The signboard itself was so encrusted with yellow dirt and bird droppings that at first it looked blank. But when Prospero had scraped some of the filth away from the warped board, he could read the fading black letters: FIVE DIALS.

"Five Dials sounds interesting," he said aloud. "But how far, for heaven's sake?"

One end of the sign was carved into an arrow, but the other end was ragged, as if a part of it had rotted or broken off. The missing piece might have told the mileage, but if there was such a piece crumbling in the mud and nettles at the side of the road, Prospero could not find it. After several minutes of match striking and weed stamping in the mosquito-infested darkness, he straightened up, gave a loud "Phah," and walked on down the road. But he had not gone a mile when he was very pleasantly surprised by the sight of the village lights, tiny yellow blots glowing in the valley ahead. From the hilltop where he stood, Prospero could see a cozy little cluster of thatched roofs, slate roofs, gables, and copper chimney pots. Over the huddled houses rose the pentagonal clock tower that gave the town its name. The shining dials said ten past seven, but the clock, picturesquely out of order, clanged hoarsely seven times as Prospero stood on the hilltop and listened. He laughed to himself and started down the gently sloping hill into the valley, whistling an old Scotch piping tune.

A few minutes later, Prospero was standing in one of the narrow streets of the little town, looking for someone who could direct him to an inn. Everyone seemed to be indoors, probably having late supper. Pots clattered and people

laughed in the distance. Prospero wandered around the town, and as he passed the rear of the humped stone church, he noticed that one of the clock faces was missing. The other four glowed like little moons, but the fifth was a black hole.

"Ought to change the town's name," he chuckled as he kicked a pebble down the street.

At last he saw a villager coming. Straight up the middle of the cobbled street tottered a comical-faced little old man, who stopped and smiled fatuously at Prospero. The two stood in silence for a minute, and then Prospero spoke.

"I beg your pardon, but could you recommend a good inn here in town?"

The old man pointed his crooked cane toward a shadowy side street and worked his jaws a couple of times before speaking. When he did speak, it was in a wheezy voice.

"Well, ye'd have yer best luck at the Card Player. Go down that alley and turn right. Ye'll see the sign. Mern crost brig."

Prospero cupped his ear. "What was that last thing you said?"

The old man looked flustered and shook his head, mumbling.

" 'S no matter. G'by. Dirks in cairn."

He hustled unsteadily on, turned the corner, and was gone.

"Funny old man," said Prospero. "Well, I hope his instructions were right."

The wizard walked briskly through the dark alley, dodging a small dog that plunged past him. In the next street, which was better lit than the other, he saw at once that the old man had not been wrong. Between two dark shops with high scalloped false fronts was a slate-roofed two-story inn.

The four green windows on the first floor were whorled and spiraled with light, and from within came the clatter of silverware and the clank of pewter mugs on wooden tables. As Prospero paused under the gently swinging signboard, he noticed the picture on it: a conjuror with four cards face down before him on a table. The fifth he held up, and it was blank.

Prospero rapped on the brass-fitted door with his staff. Almost immediately the door opened and a bar of light streamed into the street. A slightly plump middle-aged woman in an apron stood half in shadow, holding the door. Prospero could see enough of her bland round face to see that she was smiling kindly.

"Welcome!" she said. "You look like a weary traveler. Take a seat near the fire! Either fire! Would you like something to drink?"

Prospero, delighted by the hospitable air of the hostess, entered and found himself in a long smoky common room with a fireplace at either end. There were blazing wall torches, and, overhead, wheel-shaped chandeliers with dripping white candles hung by chains from the square oak beams. Prospero took out his stubby brier pipe, lit it from the fireplace, and settled on a stool near a little group of quietly talking people. The hostess brought him a cold sweating tankard of ale, and he leaned forward to catch the conversation near him.

As the evening wore on—and "wore" was the proper word—Prospero found himself more and more dissatisfied with his surroundings. The place was dull, no doubt about it. For instance, the conversation he had tried to take part in was curiously vague and listless. The people welcomed him and seemed to be cordial, but everyone was—how should he put it?—saying the same thing in different ways. He would have blessed a monologist and was tempted to become one himself, but he felt helpless in the face of this balanced, trivial buzzing. There were no rip-roaring tale tellers, and no one was bold enough to introduce a song, bawdy or otherwise.

Prospero took to looking around the room. Again, his immediate instinct was to find fault. The large brown tapestry near the door was supposed to show a hunt, but the animal being gored by the spears of the two riders was crudely done; it looked more like a man in a lion suit. The opposite wall was large, smooth, and blank. No ornaments of any kind. The candlestick on one end of the nearer mantelpiece was not matched by a mate at the other end. And in the stone front of the fireplace was an escutcheon with a dagger carved on it in low relief. Prosaic. The blank card, when you thought about it, pretty well suited this dreary place. Maybe it was under new management and things were not yet organized. That would explain the sign. The card had held some device of the previous owner's that was now painted over, and apparently the new proprietor hadn't decided what to call the place. Well, at least the food was not bad. Roast beef and Cheddar cheese and more ale. But it *is* blasted boring in here!

Prospero's thoughts ran this way the rest of the evening. The other guests left, in twos and threes, some of them going upstairs to bed. He sat practically alone now, blowing smoke rings. A little magic, perhaps some indoor lightning or stone smoke rings dropped in people's soup. That might have salvaged the evening. On the other hand, the dour people of this tavern might have responded with pained looks and silence. "Oh, another magician, how tedious! There was one in here last week, etc." Prospero laughed aloud at this train of thought, startling a man at the other end of the room, who turned, glared at him, and walked out without a word.

Soon Prospero was alone in the long room—alone except for the hostess, who was passing among the tables collecting plates and mugs. He called out to her through the stale drifting smoke.

"Madam! Are there any rooms left for the night?"

She turned and smiled vaguely. "Of course. I'll take your bag upstairs and open the bed. Stay up as long as you like."

"Thank you, but I think I'll go to my room now. It must be nearly twelve, and I am very tired."

"Very well."

Prospero pushed through the empty chairs and found his carpetbag, which he had left near the door. He waited until the hostess had put out all the downstairs lights, and then he followed her as she led the way, candle in hand, up the dully gleaming oak steps. There was a mirror in a black oval frame halfway up the stairs, and as he passed it, hardly looking at it, something about it struck him as strange. He was about to turn on the stairs, but he shrugged and went on up.

The hostess gave him the candle as they reached his room.

"Here you are, sir. Sleep well." And with that she turned and walked on down the long hall, a glimmering white figure that was soon lost in the musty shadows. Prospero stood watching her go, and then he opened his door. The room looked pleasant enough, if sparsely furnished: a small double feather bed with high sideboards; a table and chair, the latter rush-bottomed; and a long low chest with a little carved strongbox on the top. Prospero put on his nightshirt and stood at the window, smoking a last pipe. The overcast that had hidden the moon and stars was gone now, and the full moon was so bright that for a minute he could not see the features of the appalled face it always wore. Melancholy, something more than the usual sadness of silent rooms, was creeping over him as he stood there looking down at the gray-shining street. He didn't know why he felt so sad, though he suspected that the lugubrious evening he had spent downstairs was at fault. Well, to bed. He knocked out his pipe into a small lead jar. Just before he got into bed, Prospero happened to glance at the long pitchfork shadow cast on the moonlit floor by a three-branched candelabrum that was on the window sill. The shadow appeared to be wavering slightly. Prospero leaned over the bedside and stared. The shadow was still. He looked at the candlestick, then rolled over to sleep.

But he did not sleep. Prospero stared at the empty whitewashed ceiling and felt himself grow more nervous hour by hour. The five- (or four-) dialed clock struck one and two and three. And then four—the fourth stroke fell with almost a thudding sound. Wretched clock! Wretched people in this dull dead town! Prospero got up and paced about the room. Something was stirring in his mind and he could not put it together. Idly he picked up the small walnut strongbox and tried to open it. It didn't even rattle. The heart-shaped brass lock plate on the front was smooth to his touch. It had no keyhole. He turned the box over, looking for hidden locks and spring releases, but there was nothing. Prospero set the box down with a loud crack that startled him in the silent room. Strange thoughts began to come to him now: locked boxes and empty rooms. Four dials and a black hole. Four cards and a blank. And a dead sound on the stroke of four. *Why did that mirror bother him?*

Quietly Prospero got dressed, took his staff from the corner, and opened the door of his room. The hall was dark and silent. No night lamp burned at the head of the gaping stairway. He fished his metal matchbox out of an inside pocket and struck a light. On a hall table was a squat candle in a dish. He lit it and tiptoed down the stairs to the place where the mirror hung. Prospero stared and felt a chill pass through his body. The mirror showed nothing—not his face, not his candle, not the wall behind him. All he saw was a black glassy surface.

Fighting down rising fear, Prospero went back upstairs and began to knock on doors, at first softly, then sharply. He tried the doors. Locked. Locked. And locked. Like the box, the doors didn't even rattle. On an impulse, he opened his pocket knife and tried to slide the blade into the space between a door and its jamb. The point struck solid wood, for what looked like a crack was merely a black line. One door opened, revealing a completely empty room, without even a bed on its smooth floor. The window was open and a cold autumn wind blew in. Prospero shut the door quietly. At the other end of the long straight corridor was a room he had intentionally passed by. The gold letters on the door said "Innkeeper. Please knock."

"Very well," he said through his teeth. "I'll knock."

He struck the floor with his staff, and a loud report crashed through the hall. There was no echo, and the silence returned. Prospero walked slowly to the other end of the corridor until he stood before the lettered door. Placing his hand on the curved handle, he pressed down and the latch clicked. The door opened about a foot and struck something soft. Prospero raised his candle and saw that the door was blocked by the form of the hostess, who was standing in the dark room, her back to him and her arms at her sides. He squeezed through the door and held the light close to the inert form. Her head was bowed slightly and her eyes were open. His gaze wandered to her right arm. Her clenched hand was pressed to her thigh, and she clutched something hidden in the folds of her floor-length checkered skirt. Slowly, cautiously, Prospero backed away, and when he had reached the middle of the room, he glanced quickly around. The weak candlelight did not reach the dark corners, but the room looked as empty as the one he had just been in. He muttered something and struck the butt of his staff on the floor. The room lit up for an instant in a flash of blue lightning, and Prospero could see that the chamber was indeed empty—there was not even a window.

And still the woman stood silent, staring with dead eyes at the floor. Prospero bent to set the candle down, and then, straightening up suddenly, he walked to where the slumping figure stood. Grasping her shoulders, he shook her violently. There was a clatter on the floor at his feet, and when he looked down he saw a long, slightly curved butcher knife. He looked up at the woman again and stepped back with a gasp. His hand went to his face and his staff fell to the floor. The woman's eyes were gone. In her slowly rising head were two black holes. Prospero saw in his mind a doll that had terrified him when he was a child. The eyes had rattled in the china skull. Now the woman's voice, mechanical and heavy: "Why don't you sleep? Go to sleep." Her mouth opened wide, impossibly wide, and then the whole face stretched and writhed and yawned in the faint light.

With a cry Prospero shoved the melting thing aside and got to the door, opened it, and ran down the hall. The walls were caving, bulging, stretching wildly—one door fell before him and tried to wrap itself around his legs. Prospero kicked at the door hysterically and finally got to the stairs, which were covered with a brown fog. As he felt his way down the quivering steps, the whole staircase gave way with a rushing hiss and he landed on his knees in the cold liquid that had been the floor. The walls of the large downstairs room, though blurry, were still there, and he felt for the door, not daring to look back to see if anything had followed him from that terrible blind chamber. Lifting the twisting, bucking bar from the black door, he plunged outside and ran through the street, where the cobblestones oozed like mud and slate roofs turned to dripping black slime. Stone walls ran in viscous rivulets, and the head of the little old man appeared gabbling fiercely. When Prospero got to the church, the bell tower rang five scraping, cracking, howling notes and toppled slowly at him. He raised his arms to shield himself, but the tower, still ringing, turned to mist as it fell and blew away in long sinuous swirls. The wizard dropped to the ground, covering his face with his hands.

When he looked up several minutes later he was in a field of heavily trampled moonlit grass, through which a rutty gouged cowpath wandered. Some distance away the road he had been following wound up a pine-covered ridge. Near him, Prospero found his bag and staff, unharmed, and he picked them up from the withered weeds as if he expected them to crumble in his grasp. Something was glittering in the gray tangle at his feet—the knife, which was quite real, and very ordinary-looking. No inscriptions on it, no death's heads. Prospero broke it, buried it, and started walking toward the road.

SEVEN

On his way again, Prospero crossed ridge after ridge of uninteresting country: a cattle pond here, a clump of Scotch pines there—just enough variation for boredom. He was beginning to feel that this was a pointless, hopeless journey. The situation, the problem that faced him, was getting clearer in his mind, and the clearer it got, the more hopeless he felt. Without Roger he was lost.

After half a day of walking, something happened that made him strangely hopeful. He found a sign, a fairly new sign, that said FIVE DIALS: THIRTY MILES. So there *was* a town with that name, after all. He walked the rest of the day, stopped to build a fire in a little circle of pines, and slept a full nine hours. The next morning, after coffee, bread, and cheese, he went on, feeling much better.

Five Dials, it turned out, was not a town at all, but a

lonely inn wedged under a yellow limestone bank, a last friendly stop before you reached the Brown River and the treeless empty moors of the North Kingdom. A man by the name of Clockwarden had been here first, in the barn-shaped house that was still the center of the collection of different-sized, plugged-together buildings that made up the Five Dials Inn. Clockwarden may not have been his real name, since that was his job. On the cliff over the inn stood a crenelated clock tower, built some two hundred years before the time of this story; it was the hobby work of some local prince, and it had had, when new, four brightly painted wooden dials with keyhole-shaped windows cut in them. Through these you could see moons and suns rising and setting—not that they ever told you anything about moonrise, sunrise, or the tides. The fifth dial was a sundial on the flat top of the tower; it was used to set the clock, which had only hour hands. After the prince who built the clock died, his successors let the thing run down and dismissed the warden. They tore off the bronze hands and made them into spearheads; the lead weights were thrown off a castle wall in some forgotten siege.

Two days after his escape from Five Dials, Prospero stood on Clocktower Hill, looking up at warped, bleached, saucer-shaped faces that still had a few flaking Roman numerals. Inside, the works were full of birds' nests—empty at this time of year—and in some places small skeletons were caught in cogs, because playing children or a strong wind had started the rope-and-stone pendulum and the big square-toothed wooden wheels. From the Clocktower Hill you could see, to the north, a valley of little jigsaw-puzzle fields cut up by bunchy and badly trimmed hedgerows. Beyond the fields was a curving fence of tall feather-shaped trees that marked the course of the Brown River, the border between the North and South kingdoms. The road that ran past the inn must meet a bridge at that point. It was near sunset, and Prospero watched for a while as a stone-blue point of cloud, rising out of a thick curded mass, cut the red sun in two. Suppertime at the inn. Two maple trees grew at the western edge of the low cliff and marked the place where the stone steps led down to the side yard of the inn. As Prospero passed between the trees, a little breeze started and a leaf scraped his cheek. He felt a sharp pain and blood wet his face. Reaching up carefully and staring hard at the dark moving leaves, he broke one off at the stem and held it up in the light. It was not hard—it was unpleasantly soft and furry feeling, like a caterpillar. Its edges and veins were gray, and it had turned a dark red. With a nervous look over his shoulder, Prospero hurried down the steps.

Inside the inn was a pleasant reeky disorder, with a gonglike whanging of kettles, loud talk, and some shouting. This place seemed real enough. The tables had pipe-ash burns and interlaced bottle marks; the mantel was crowded with smudged mustard jars, dirty boot-shaped leather pitchers, and speckled china jam pots. Bent and tarnished spoons stood upright in some thick green stuff that dripped over the edges of dirty white porcelain bowls. Lifting his bag over the heads of ducking customers, Prospero squeezed through the tables and found the innkeeper. He wanted a glass of wine before supper, and he had heard—all the way back in Brakespeare—that the cellars of the border inns were very good, especially for port and sherry. "Go on down and help yourself," said the fat blue-aproned man. "Here's a glass. You won't need a candle; the place is all lit up. Don't drink too much, ha ha."

"I won't, ha ha," said Prospero to himself, and he started down the stairs.

In the cellar, rows of splintery tarred barrels ran off into the vaulted alleys; here and there lumpy starfish-shaped grease lamps gave off a smudgepot stink and precious little light. Prospero looked around and saw a man in a brown robe bent over a little low barrel. He was turning the spigot and drawing off a thick brown fluid that was probably sherry. Prospero stood watching him from a distance, and the man started to talk in a creaky old-geezer voice. It was not clear if he was talking to himself, but he gave no sign that he knew the other man was there.

"Ye-es, this is proper Snake Year sherry, it is. I've got the right barrel. *Snake* Year, ye say? Thaat's right, thaat's right. Seems they was a plague of adders several years ago. Well, they come down off of that Clock Hill lookin' for a cold dark place, and they filled this cellar up to the gunnels. Right up to the roof beams. Wrigglin' and squirmin' like anything. Well, old whatsisname come down here in a suit of armor he borrowed up the road, and he laid around with a broadsword till they was all dead. Well, then they aired out the cellar 'n' carted out the *segments,* or figments if ye please"—here he broke down into shaking silent laughter and hit his head several times against the barrel rim—"but it took 'em a long time to get this funny *smell* out. They finally did, most of it, but this here barrel, if ye pop out the bung, still smells bracky. That's because a lady adder set down some eggs in here. She *squirmed* in the spigot and she *squirmed* out again. Now they ain't many that *likes* this barrel, but *I* claim the taste is special."

All the while that this strange old man was talking, Prospero was walking toward him through the rows of kegs.

Now he stood directly behind the stooping hooded figure.

"Are you serious?" said Prospero. "About that?"

"I am," said the old man. "Here—*try some!*" He screeched these last words, straightened up suddenly, and shoved the slopping mug in Prospero's face. The wizard's reaction was automatic, as if he had had a dead rat thrown in his lap. He jerked back, swung his arm, and batted the mug across the room. It bounced on kegs with a dull *tunk-tunk,* spewing brown wine everywhere. Prospero stood staring at the old man, who was Roger Bacon.

"Oh, good grief! Roger, if you ever do that again, I'll make you drink real snake wine, it's a very simple formula, you just . . ." Now he was crying, with his arms around the red-bearded man.

"Roger, how did you know I'd be here? How did you know I'd come down here?"

"I was watching you from the top of that ridiculous tower. Did you think I was the gnomon, in the shape of Father Time?"

"I didn't see you."

"Well, I saw you miles off. I went to Briar Hill and saw your mark in the guest book. I didn't know where you'd go after that, but I went north for reasons of my own, and figured you'd come for the same reasons."

"Don't be mysterious," said Prospero. "What reasons? And how did you happen to go to Briar Hill? And what happened . . ."

"Better not to talk down here," said Roger, staring around at the barrels. "Let's get a back parlor with a nice thick door on it. We can take turns talking."

The two of them sat, later in the evening, at a scallop-edged wooden table on which four gray squares of bright

moonlight lay. In the corner a little fire of pine chunks burned behind a thick iron grate pierced with quatrefoils. On the table were two greasy tin plates, a couple of half-full mugs of cider, and a squashed-down tallow candle in a green copper dish. A brass cylinder marked "Salt" held thick peeling cigars—the innkeeper rolled them himself—and Prospero lit one from the candle. Roger was trying to light a bulbous black pipe that looked like an avocado on a stick. Smoke, swirling in graceful slow strands, drifted toward the field-stone chimney.

"All right," said Prospero. "You go first. What happenened?"

"Well," said Roger, "I was sitting on the stump, smoking, just as I am now, and the first odd thing I noticed was the Hall of Records. It looked strange, as if the moon were shining on it and not on anything else. It should have been in shadow, with those oak trees and pines all around, and besides, it must have been overcast. But I didn't think of that. I stared at the door, and then it opened, and you—or someone I thought was you—came out. You walked up to me and grabbed my arm, and your hand seemed to be made out of frozen sticks. 'Come on,' you said. 'We've got to get away from here.' So I followed you off into the forest, and when we were deep inside you shriveled with a sound like several voices holding the same dead note. All that was left was a log made of ashes—as if a piece of wood had burned all the way through while keeping its original shape. I didn't know what to do. At first I thought that the wizard with the book had finally got you; I wept, raged, and beat on trees with my fists. When I was exhausted I realized that I was lost. I had left my compass in my bag, which was back at the stump with my staff. So I sat under a big ugly elm all night, and in the morning I found my way back to the Hall. My bag and staff had been pulled into some brambles, and you, of course, were gone. I went in and read the passage in the Register. It wasn't hard to find, because you had propped the book open."

"What did you think when you read it?" Prospero was staring at him with a pained smile.

"I was surprised to see Melichus' name. It looks as though he was the foreigner who took the book from the monk at Glastonbury. If the Register is right, Melichus deserved his death."

"He's not dead."

Roger dropped the avocado pipe into the tin plate, making a sound that startled both of them. He looked at Prospero's long moonlit face as if he might be another ghost, or Melichus himself.

Prospero knew what Roger was thinking, and he started to laugh. "No, I'm not Melichus or a log traveling incognito. But he *is* alive."

"I didn't really think you were he," said Roger, blushing a little. "But how did he escape from that blazing forest?"

"He never was in it. Go on, though. Why did you go to Briar Hill if you thought Melichus was dead?"

"I thought some assistant might have taken the book after the mob . . ."

"You're close," said Prospero.

"I can see you have *your* revelations," said Roger. "Anyway, I went to Briar Hill, but it took me about two days because I got on the wrong road. Did you know that I left my map-book on your kitchen table? Mrs. Durfey is probably using it to wrap sandwiches in. Where was I? Oh yes. I got to Briar Hill and found your mark at the Gorgon's Head.

Nicholas Archer indeed. I could have done better. Why not say you were Bishop Lanfranc?"

"I left my miter in the closet," said Prospero. "Go on."

"Well, I paid my bill at the inn and went to the ruins of Melichus' cottage to see what I could see, and I spent several hours poking around among rotten timbers and broken glass. The floor had fallen through, and I could see there was a basement, so I went down—the steps are still there—and I found a door under some half-burned boards. Just a door, not hidden like the one in your root cellar, but for the same purpose. I doubt if the villagers have noticed it, because they probably haven't touched the place, except to paint curses on the walls. At any rate, the door opened into a tunnel. Not a vaulted and decorated one like yours, but a low muddy thing with roots sticking through the ceiling. You have to go all the way down bent over. After a little while I saw light, but not daylight. Thin moonlight, wavery, like northern lights. Remember, this was no later than four in the afternoon. I came out into a little grove of trees by a pond. It was winter. Black ice with little animals frozen into it just below the surface. From their look they had been trying to get out. Trees bent over to the ground by ice, and overhead, in a flat black sky, a featureless moon. I stood there by the edge of the pond for quite some time, and then I heard a thin little crack at the far end. I saw a jagged pencil line start in the ice. It ran—and ran is the right word—across the pond, swerving a little but headed for me. Before it got to the bank where I had been standing, I was halfway up the tunnel. I don't think anyone can reach that place without going through that passage."

"I'll be happy if I never find it," said Prospero, and he looked out the window at the rising moon, which, fortunately, had a face. "What did you do after that?"

"I decided to spend another night at the inn, and that is what convinced me that I ought to go north. At first the people at the inn were a little scared of me. I gather you gave them some kind of fright. But they decided that I was a monk, and that I had come to exorcise the cottage, so everything went well. That is, they talked to me in the common room that night. But the talk was not comfortable. There were several travelers there from the north, and they were convinced that witches were at work in their towns. What worried me most was the kind of story they told. Not the usual things of wells being poisoned, toads found in beds, ghosts rapping at windows. They talked about signboards creaking in the wind, trees casting odd shadows, dark cellarways that used to scare only children. And cloaks fluttering, and moths brushing faces in dark rooms. I tried to sleep that night, but I couldn't, so I packed up, left a few coins on the bed—not in the fireplace—and headed north. I was given a ride by a hay wagon, and got ahead of you that way, I guess. But even then you must have stopped along the way."

"Yes," said Prospero. "I was detained. Let me tell you about it."

Without any of his usual storyteller's flair, Prospero told Roger what had happened: the feverish night in the Hall of Records, the stone and the fire, and the marks on his door at the Gorgon's Head. He gave a short and very reticent description of what had happened in the Empty Forest, and an account of the Five Dials incident that was very vague, so vague that Roger had to keep asking him questions about his experience. After Prospero had finished, he went over to the fire and started poking it.

"So Melichus has the book," said Roger. "And he sent his

apprentice out to face the mob while he got out the back way."

"Yes," said Prospero, with his back to Roger. "And now we know why he wants to kill me."

"We do? If *you* do, tell me, for heaven's sake!"

Prospero looked very surprised when he turned around. "You mean to say that I never told you? I thought of it immediately when I saw Melichus' name in the Register. That's why I had to find out if he was alive."

"Tell me," said Roger, exasperated, "or do I have to put you to the Inquisitorial Question?"

"I'm sorry," said Prospero, smiling. "I didn't mean to be so suspenseful. It's the green-glass paperweight."

Roger stared. "I know sorcerers aren't supposed to be ignorant, but *what* is the green-glass paperweight?"

Prospero sat down. "It all started when Melichus and I were learning magic from Michael Scott. You knew *that*, didn't you?"

"Yes, yes. Don't be sarcastic."

"Well, before we could be initiated into the order, we had to spend several months living together in a lonely valley in the mountains up north. We lived in a cottage that is still there, as far as I know, though I haven't visited the place since we left all those years ago. I imagine there's a whole village up there now. The grass is good for sheep. At any rate, our final task was to make something together, some little magic object put together by our combined powers. It wasn't easy working with Melichus, and we quarreled several times before we finished. He always enjoyed doing things by himself, and as soon as we were through, he left with a 'Well, that's over!' look at me. I never saw him again."

"What did you make?"

"We made a little green-glass thing. I usually think of it as a paperweight, because that's what I'd use it for if I had it at home. I dream about it sometimes. It is made of four transparent green globes. Three of them always show snow falling in some desolate and, to my mind, sinister little place. Neither of us knew where it was. A road crossing with high banks, bare trees, and a leaning stone marker at the place where the roads meet. It always looked, or rather felt, as though someone were about to come up one of the roads. But no one ever did. The fourth globe could be used as a conventional seeing glass, though it showed only places that you knew about or had visited. Melichus lost interest in it almost as soon as we had finished it."

"Why didn't you take it with you? Competition wouldn't hurt that insufferable mirror of yours."

"I couldn't take it, and neither could Melichus. The night before we were to put the final spell on it, we both dreamed the same dream. In it we were told that the thing could not be taken from the house unless the two of us took it together, each actually touching it with his hand. And then we could never let it go if we wanted to keep it. It would be like being chained together. Neither of us knows—unless *he* has found out somehow—what would happen if one of us tried to take it away."

"What would happen if one of you died?"

"The other would get the thing. He could take it away, if he felt like going all the way up into the mountains of the North Kingdom for what may be only a magician's toy. But I'm sure he doesn't think it's just a toy, and I don't either. I told you that I dream about it. And sometimes when I'm traveling in the winter, I come to a place that looks a lot like the one in the glasses. I get the strangest feeling, and I wait a moment to see if something will happen. Nothing does, but the feeling is very odd."

"I still don't see," said Roger, "why he would want to kill you because of that thing."

Prospero looked nervously out the window, as if he expected to see Melichus coming up the moonlit road toward the inn.

"Think," he said, "of all the years—fifty now—that he has been learning to use that terrible book. Think of the things he must have done. It has meant giving up all the rest of his life, anything else that he might have been doing before he started to decipher those words. And he's alone. I'm almost certain he has no human help now. He has those things he has sent to terrify me, but I doubt if they are much company. If anyone had a share in what he was doing, he would be afraid that the sharer would try to steal the book, or burn it, or use it against him. Well, *I* have a share in his power, through that little piece of glass, the magic object that I might be able to use against him. I might be able to wipe out all his work. The idea of it must make his thoughts murderous."

"Why didn't he kill you at the Hall, then?"

"I don't think he could, yet. The cloak, the moth, and those things in gray might have scared me to death, but I'm sure now that they couldn't have hurt me. Or you. The painted stone and the fire are black magic, as you well know. Good old-fashioned black magic. But I am still strong enough to undo spells. Some spells. The 'village' of Five Dials was beyond my powers."

"He may have given up on you for the time being," said Roger. "From what I heard at Briar Hill he must be going on with his original plans. We can hope that he has lost track of you."

"I hope so. We've got to get to that cottage, though I can imagine what he has waiting for us there. He is getting terribly strong. Have you ever seen anything like this?"

Prospero reached carefully into his pocket and brought out the gray-veined maple leaf. It lay there for a few seconds in the candlelight, and then it started to crawl like a worm, humping in the middle and then straightening out. Roger grabbed it and held it in the flame, where it twisted and blackened into a sticky tar lump. He walked across the room and threw the thing into the fire.

"I've seen those trees on the hill," he said. "And I've seen more on the road. All the trees are beginning to turn, and it's only the first of September. It's cold, too, for this time of year. I think we had better get started tomorrow."

In his room, a tilting, hump-floored box in the second-story overhang, Prospero stood by the window while the warming pan was heating his sheets. His hand scraped against a crusty iron bracket that held an old prayerbook. Something for those guests with night fears. The book, by now a foxed clump of loose leaves, was held together by a piece of cloth tied around the middle. Prospero pulled loose the bowknot and turned over the pages. He knew all the prayers, and he knew that most of them were useless unless you knew the right place to put the stresses and what the notes of the chant should be. A real magician could shake the walls with some of them. With a quick push, Prospero unstuck the little window. Down below, the road ran past the front door of the inn. He chose the famous prayer that contains the phrase "*negotium perambulans in tenebris,*" and he began to sing it in a loud voice, rising to held high notes at the middle and the end of each line. He got his answer. Out of the dark willow thicket opposite the inn a little cloud of dead leaves flew. They spun a dusty whirlwind in the middle of the road, until one shot up at Prospero's open window. His hand was on the latch, and the slamming of the black wooden frame was instantly followed by a *splat*. The leaf slid down the window, streaking it with the wet sticky gobs of an insect's innards.

EIGHT

Around two in the morning, Prospero woke up, and his feet were on the cold floor before he knew what had awakened him. Downstairs someone was pounding on the big front door. They were heavy resonant blows, not made with a fist but with something harder, like the butt end of a sword. Resisting the urge to throw open the window and shout insults, Prospero got up and looked through the glass. He had been about to light a candle, but he put it down now and opened the window slowly so that he could hear what was being said. There were soldiers down there, mail-shirted pikemen in rusty soup-plate helmets. They carried saw-toothed bills, blunt-ended broadswords, maces, and battle-axes. Even in the waning moonlight Prospero could see that their equipment was dirty and corroded; some of the pike points were cockeyed, and only half of the men—there were fifty altogether that he could see—wore coats of arms of any kind. Those that did had the badly sewn-on emblems of some local ruler, a shield with three Greek crosses and a hatchet. Now there was a scraping of bolts as the innkeeper opened up. The man who had been doing the pounding—Prospero could not see him because of the overhang—shouted.

"All right, men! Come on in. A few drinks and then we've got work!"

The pikemen, some of them hawking and spitting loudly, clattered in after their leader. Outside Prospero's door there was a small staircase that led down to a dark pantry full of brackish-smelling empty barrels. The wooden partition of the service window was slid back just a bit, and through it Prospero saw the stamping grouchy soldiers sloshing beer from stoneware jugs into their tankards. The leader was dumping coins into the cupped hands of the sleepy-eyed innkeeper, who asked what was going on.

"We're going over to the north to burn that town . . . Bow . . . what's its name?"

"Bishops Bowes," said the innkeeper. "Why are you doing this?"

"We've finally figured out what's going on. Town's full of evil people. Witches. I have an order here from Duke Harald to burn it to the ground. Here, look at it. Not that you have anything to say in this."

He unrolled a long parchment that trailed lead and yellow wax seals on twisted strings of skin. The signature, a cross with a letter on each point, was so large that it covered a quarter of the page.

"They deserve it, too," the leader went on. "You've seen the things. Half the people in Wellfont are afraid to go down into their own cellars. Shadows moving, screams from kettles when there isn't any fire. Well, a little fire'll teach 'em. A couple of my men are out getting wood for torches. Do you have any pitch?"

"In the basement. I use it on the roof."

"That's fine. We're going to use it on the roof too." He laughed, spitting flecks of brown beer on the muddy floor.

Prospero did not wait any longer. He climbed the steep stairs quietly, hands on the dark steps in front of him, and soon he was shaking Roger awake.

"Come on. They're going to burn the village. How far is Bishops Bowes?"

Roger sat up. "Uh? Hah? Bishops Bowes? Five miles. There's a bridge; that's why it's called Bishops Bowes. 'Bowes' are the arches of a bridge. Wait till I get dressed."

In a few minutes the two wizards were opening one of the several side doors of the inn. A cold beaded lamp on a curved hook hung over them, and a few late fall insects clung to the mottled glass. Each man could see how nervous the other looked.

"Well," said Prospero, whispering, "have we got everything?"

"I thing so. Let's hope those louts stay here for a while. We will have to walk fast."

And they did walk fast. For old men, Roger and Prospero could really travel on foot if they had to, and before long the noisy inn with its clattering cans and torchlight was far behind. In a rising wind that thrashed the nearby bare bushes by the roadside, they hiked down the gravelly strip of yellow clay. There was the bridge, a long flattened arch of close-fitted unmortared stones. Bishop Hatto's arms were carved in relief on the keystone faces. Trickling moss hung over his moons and dogs' heads, and his miter was trimmed with stars of yellow stonecrop. At each end of this wide bridge sat a pair of stone wardens, giant Norse chessmen in high backed chairs, hunched gloomy kings with swords on their knees. The keepers of the Bishop's Bridge sat staring with deep-drilled empty pupils. Prospero hung his hat on one of them.

"Well, here we are. Roger, you'd better go ahead and get the townspeople out of bed. You know the people around here and I don't. Don't scare them too much. I think I can keep these clots at a distance for a while."

Roger walked out onto the bridge and looked over the side. Fast water hissed around the back marble pillars. Little clusters of bubbles moved downstream.

"I hate to say this," said Roger, "but I think you'd better destroy this bridge. I've been thinking about some things on the way here. Harald is one of the few southern kings with a real following, and he is also one of the few who think looting and burning are manly sports. There'll be more soldiers before we get rid of Melichus, if we can. And there are no stone bridges for three hundred miles either way. We can count on the Northerners on the border to burn the wooden bridges if it looks like war."

"I guess you're right. Very well, I'll meet you when this business is over. And this time, don't turn into a monster."

"I'll try not to. Good luck." Roger waved and walked across the bridge, clicking his staff on the rough stones of the railing.

Now that Prospero was alone, he found that he wanted to smoke. Out came the stubby brier and the tin matchbox with the nutmeg-grater sides. *Brrrip!* went the match, and it shot little pinsparks before flaming an acrid yellow. Prospero lit his pipe and threw the match into the water, where it sank like a nail. It gave a skyrockety *ka-foosh*, and the whole river under and around the bridge was lit up. Awakened fish swam in little flipping darts and a turtle started to swim toward the surface. Prospero was leaning over the rail and laughing at the idiocy and essential triviality of a wizard who made magic matches. He laughed until he realized that he hadn't the faintest idea of how to destroy a bridge.

And now the soldiers were coming. He could hear them clanking and stomping, and over the black horizon was a bouncing orange glimmer. They must be about two hills away, he thought. Bridges. How to destroy a bridge. No time to go riffling through the book, and anyway he knew he wouldn't find anything there. Tarot cards? Ha! Well, it was worth a try, and from the sounds up the road he would only have one try. He dug into the bag and brought out a pack of tarot cards in a painted cardboard case. But which ones to use? Some sort of logic had to be followed, and it would take several years to try all possible combinations. What about the four aces at the corners and the tower struck by lightning in the center? All right, but hurry!

He ran from one corner of the bridge to the other. Using candle wax to hold down the cards, he put the aces of cups, coins, staves, and swords on the four rail ends of the bridge. The wind had died down, so it was easy to hold the cards in place. A whack of his hand squashed the pasteboard against the wax. Now he was in the middle of the bridge again, holding the tower card that signifies madness and destruction. He pasted it to the center of the bridge, on the pentagonal block that lined up with the two keystones. Stamping on the card with his heel, he shouted:

"Bridge, *break!*
Stones, *crack!*"

He was not surprised when nothing happened. The dirty straw-covered stones were still in place. The fern-capitaled marble columns that Bishop Hatto had stolen from a church still held up their load. And the soldiers were coming.

They were at the top of the hill that looked down on the bridge. A cluster of shiny bloodflashed kettles with dark bristled faces underneath. Tipping pike poles and pendulum-swaying chain maces. Prospero stood and watched them come. They probably can't see me yet, he thought, with those blazing torches and a moonless night. He walked to the rail and relit his pipe. The troop halted at the edge of the bridge with a dishpan clatter. Their leader squinted into the darkness for a minute, and then he handed his torch to someone. He drew his sword, a plain iron blade without bosses or jewels. Now his feet were clumping on the pavement.

Prospero felt the ragged blade point touch his beard.

"Well, old man, what are you doing here?"

"Looking at the fish, an it please Your Lordship." Prospero tipped his hat and blew smoke out of the corners of his mouth.

"Really? In the dark? You'll be able to see them better from the bottom of the river."

"Ah, but I won't be able to smoke in all that wet, will I?"

Prospero raised his arm and threw his pipe on the stones, where it burst with a sudden red flash that lit the faces of the two men. A second after came an aerial-bomb thud that hurt the ears of everyone standing near. The leader's sword flew into the air and came down looking like a big buttonhook. He ran back, holding his ears, and little corkscrewing ribbons of fire screeched after the army, as they turned into a colliding, shouting metal thicket that hustled away down the road.

Prospero stood there wishing that he knew how to destroy bridges. An image came back that had registered in his

116

mind when he first saw the bridge. One of the staring stone wardens had a little crack around his neck. Prospero ran to the figure, pulled off the head, and with a sudden heave threw it off the bridge. The carved lump hit the mud with a thock, and now he could see a little square hole in the neck. A piece of paper was in it. Without stopping to read the charm, which might have been interesting at another time, Prospero tore it up and went back to the middle of the bridge. He tapped the card with his staff.

"Bridge, *break!*"

The mate of the headless statue pitched forward on its face, one of the mossy coats of arms fell into the stream, the pillars shook in their muddy sockets, and the bridge started to lurch in hiccupy spasms. But it did not collapse.

The soldiers were coming back now, shouting. Prospero thumped his staff as if he was churning butter, all the while shouting, "Break, blast you, break!" When the soldiers were on the bridge again, bill points lowered for a charge, they saw a sweating old man throw down his stick. He took the remaining cards from his pocket and threw them in the air. A fountain of orange-and-black strips fell around him. The cloud of cards started to whirl and a stiff streaming wind began to blow between the high curbs of the bridge, freezing the little army in the act of charging, so that for a moment it looked like a statuary group. Then they were blowing down the road, skidding on rocks and vaulting very professionally on bending pikestaffs. The wind blew them flat to the ground and kept on blowing. Five miles away the innkeeper of Five Dials was emptying a tub of dishwater in his back yard, a little alcove in the cup of the overhanging cliff. He heard a whizzing overhead and looked up to see the copper weather-

cock spinning into a blurry ball. As he watched in stupid amazement, he heard a bang out in front. Peeking around the shingled corner, he saw a helmet rocking in the road like a little round boat.

Back at the bridge, Prospero was running on a pitching stone deck. Slime-haired blocks popped up and fell into the stream. He heard a long roar and many heavy splashes behind him, and suddenly he was standing on a tipping pile of stones. One arm heaved the bag to the bank; the other threw the staff spinning into the dark grass. A standing broad jump brought him to the bank, where he fell into a clump of thistles. He rolled out of it and sat there with little forked burrs littering his robe. A shadow moved over his head as one of the stone men—there were two on this side as well—stood up on grinding stone knees, raising a thick sword in blocky fists. The glum face nodded, the knees cracked, and the statue, sitting in his chair again, slid backwards down the bank.

At Bishops Bowes, the first thing Prospero saw was Roger sitting on a keg of onions in the middle of the empty street. He was smoking and staring placidly around at empty windows.

"They're all gone," he said. "They were gone when I got here. I suppose the news got to them and they fled to some castle. How did your bridge go?"

"I'll tell you about it later," said Prospero, who was still picking burrs out of his robe. "What are we going to do now?"

"Well, I've looked around the town. There are two horses left in the stable here. I suggest that we take them and leave some money. It's a long way to the mountains, and you can feel that something is gathering. I felt it all the way up here from the bridge."

"But I can't ride a horse!" said Prospero. "You know that. I was frightened of ponies when I was a child. And it won't do you any good to give me riding lessons. I'm still scared."

"Fine figure of a wizard!" said Roger, chuckling, "Ah, me. You'll never guess what I'm going to do. Or try to do. Come on."

Roger led the way out of the little town to a thickly planted and weedy garden. The black mucky soil sprouted string beans in pale green clusters—their pods felt sticky and furry to Prospero as he bent down to look at them—the delicate ferny tops of carrots, big clumpish cabbages, and tomato vines on leaning crutches. Roger passed these by. He was looking for something else.

Prospero suddenly knew what was going on. "Oh, good heavens! Great elephantine, cloudy, adamant heavens full of thunder stones! Roger! You can't be serious. Are you?"

Roger was looking around and drumming his forefinger against his teeth. "If I were serious I would never have become a wizard, would I? The fact that it's been done before doesn't stop it from happening again. And we've got to get there somehow."

"There are no pumpkins in this garden," said Prospero. "Anyone can see that." He reached up a vine and broke off a tomato. The slippery red flesh was already getting loose and wrinkly. "Here. Work on this."

"Thanks," said Roger sourly. "We'll see. And wouldn't *you* be surprised."

"I would," said Prospero. "And I'm watching. What kind of spell are you going to use?"

"Something appropriately silly," said Roger. "Hum. Te-tum. Oh, *tum* te tum. 'Awe bleteth after lamb, lhuth after calve cu' . . . ah!"

He put the tomato down in the middle of a patch of spear-bladed weeds. Touching it with his wand, he recited calmly:

> *"Higgeldy-piggeldy*
> *Saint Athanasius*
> *Riffled through volumes*
> *In unseemly haste;*
>
> *"Trying to find out if*
> *(Hagiographically)*
> *John of Jerusalem*
> *Liked almond paste."*

At first the tomato just wobbled foolishly on its platform of weeds. Then it swelled and spun into a reddish cloud of gaseous bromine—deadly if inhaled—which gradually took the shape of a carriage. Unfortunately, it was the kind of carriage you would expect from an overripe tomato: a large sagging purse of red leather on prickly green wheels. As Prospero and Roger watched disgustedly, the wet jowly bag collapsed, oozing ketchup from many slurping cracks.

"Care for a bean?" said Prospero.

"You be quiet. Just be quiet. Look, there's more to this garden. Come on."

They walked farther in, stepping over rows of parsnips and cauliflowers. Vines, finally, and on them knobbly green-streaked yellow squashes. When Roger picked one up, he noticed that it was rotten black underneath: Yellow strings of pulp and seeds hung from the caved-in belly of the plant. One after another he turned them up, and they were all like that. He was about to give up when he saw a little streak of orange under an intricately knotted pile of vines. This squash was solid; he thubbed his staff against its goose-pimpled sides.

"This will do nicely. All right, stand back.

> *"Higgeldy-piggeldy*
> *John Cantacuzene*
> *Swaddled in Byzantine*
> *Pearl-seeded robes*
>
> *"Put out the eyes of his*
> *Iconophanical*
> *Prelate, for piercing his*
> *Priestly ear lobes."*

The squash flew into a saffron-powder rage, and when the dust settled, there was a square black Amish-style box carriage. It smelled faintly of kerosene, the leather-strap springs were cracked, but it looked serviceable. On the doors and ceiling, for some reason, were dusky paintings of river landscapes, and the black horsehair-filled upholstery had silver ashtrays set into its tufted armrests. Two bull's-eye oil lamps burned on the front.

"There!" said Roger. "Let's get those horses."

The two wizards went north. For days they rode across flat tableland where nothing but long yellowed grass and dusty goldenrod grew. In the distance you might see a tree or one of those tall watchtowers that the Northerners built. Those towers were not like anything seen in the south: Round, narrow, and with pointed stone roofs, they looked like huge candles; usually they had three floors, connected by ladders, that could be pulled up through holes in case of attack. You could not hold out for long in them if you were besieged, but a fire could be lit on the upper story and the smoke could be seen for miles. Once Prospero and Roger found one of these towers planted next to the road on which they were traveling. It was night and there were soldiers outside, sitting around a peat fire. They were not laughing, drinking, or telling stories. Instead, they sat grimly hunched over, poking the fire with their spears and wearing their acorn helmets. Long narrow nosepieces, fire-shadowed, made their faces look evil. They must have heard the carriage rattling along miles away, but none of them looked up as it rolled past, spitting gravel. They were waiting for something else.

The few scattered towns of the North were usually hidden under the lee of a low hill; or you might find houses scattered through the trees of a little grove, or grouped at the foot of a landscaped and terraced hill of farmed fields. On top there was always a castle without battlements, a long oval wall of odd-shaped heaped stones, pierced by cruciform loopholes. The carriage passed several of these dumpy forts but never came close to any of them; Prospero, using his brassbound telescope, could see that the fields were untended, and that the drawbridges were up.

In the roadside towns, the wizards picked up stories and rumors. One man told how frost formed on the windows at night, though it was only the middle of September. There were no scrolls or intricate fern leaves, no branching overlaid starclusters; instead people saw seasick wavy lines, disturbing maps that melted into each other and always seemed on the verge of some recognizable but fearful shape. At dawn the frost melted, always in the same way: At first two black eyeholes formed, and then a long steam-lipped mouth that spread and ate up the wandering white picture. In some

123

towns people talked of clouds that formed long opening mouths. One man in the town of Edgebrake sat up all night, staring at a little smiling cookie jar made in the shape of a fat monk; it stood on a high cupboard shelf, smiling darkly amid shadows. The man would not tell anyone what was wrong, or what he thought was wrong. Doors opened at night inside some houses, and still shadows that could not be cast by firelight fell across beds and floors. People who lived near forests and groves dreamed that the trees were calling to their children; in the daytime, pools of shadow that floated trembling around the trees seemed darker than they should have been, and when the children showed an unusually strong desire to play in the woods, panicked parents locked them indoors. Voices rose from empty wells, and men locked their doors at dusk.

One night, after weeks of travel, Prospero and Roger were sitting around a fire they had made near a peat bog. Orion burned cold and tilted overhead in a sky that seemed emptier than it should have been. The chill was close around them, and even in their woolen high-collared cloaks they felt that they were sitting in a wet cellar. There was none of the bracing windy cold of the empty northern fields—just clinging, bad-smelling damp. Prospero was reading his large handwritten book, and Roger, whose legs had gone numb, got up to walk around. He walked past the carriage and stopped suddenly. There was a man standing by the horses. He was wearing a coarse-spun cloak and a furry hat pulled down over his ears, and he was touching the horses with the tips of his fingers. Not petting them, just touching them to see if they were real. Roger stood there and watched him, his hand resting on the steamed-up nickel surface of one carriage lamp. When the man looked up and saw the bearded face gruesomely footlighted, he jumped back with a sucked-in yelp, as if he had slammed his hand down on a nail.

"Yes," said Roger. "I'm real, too. We won't hurt you." He was trying to look kind, but he felt more like laughing. Prospero got up and walked over to join them, his book slung under his arm.

"Then *please*, sir," said the man, "and you too, sir, will you see me home? I live five miles down the road and I'm afraid."

"Of what? Bandits?" Prospero asked the question, knowing that "bandits" would not be the answer.

"Come with me and I'll show you. You are men of magic. I am not so foolish that I can't see that. There are no carriages like this on our roads. Come with me."

All three men got into the dusty black carriage; Roger sat in the middle, holding the reins, and when they were sure they had all their gear, he clucked to the horses and the wheels swished through the tall wet weeds. The road they turned onto was a well-kept branch of the Great Way, a major highway broad enough for two wide wagons to pass; this stretch of it was bordered by a low wall of brown square-cut sandstone. The running lamplight flickered on a stone cross, one of the milestones marking the distance from the Feasting Hill to the Brown River. Rigid stone saints, their faces washed empty by rain, clung to the wheel that bound the arms of the cross together. The farmer leaned out the window and pointed at the marker.

"It's not far now. Yes, there it is!"

They stopped at the edge of a walled graveyard. In the bright moonlight a slate-roofed chapel stood under the dripping yellow leaves of a huge half-dead willow. Prospero and Roger got out and followed the farmer over a rickety wooden stile. Inside the yard were narrow roof-shaped tombs —replicas of the coffin lids that rotted below—flat, thick, ground-level slabs, and church-window-pointed uprights. Years of weathering had peeled irregular paper-thin layers from the slabs, so that the remaining letters lay in puddles and islands of flint. The farmer, kneeling, pointed to a long stone that was cracked into six or seven jagged pieces.

"Look at these. Tell me what this means, if you can."

The broken words, some filled with dark blobs of moss, said "empty," "dark," "hollow," "doomed." All the gravestones were alike. The words repeated were the same—nothing else was left.

Roger gently grasped the man's shaking arm.

"Come. We'll take you home."

As they left the churchyard, Prospero turned to look at the little chapel. The willow's limp strings were moving over the broken shingles in an ugly caressing way. There were letters on the slates:

IT IS NOT LONG TIL–

He saw that "TIL" had had two Ls—the second had slid halfway down the roof.

A few miles down the road the carriage stopped at the farmer's cottage, a whitewashed oblong topped by two lumpy haystack gables. In the two upper windows scowling jack-o'-lanterns burned—Southerners had started the custom, and it had spread among folk who thought amulets and hex signs were not enough to keep away night creatures. The Dutch door of the cottage was open at the top, and the strong-looking woman who leaned over the sill was silhouetted in orange firelight. She held, not a broom, but a short pike pole. The farmer called to her.

"It's all right, Maria, these are friends." He turned to Prospero and Roger, who were ready to drive on.

"Why don't you stay here for the night? It's well past midnight, and we have a big empty bed upstairs. Our sons grew up a long time ago."

Prospero looked at Roger. "Why not? Taking turns sleeping in that bouncing hatbox has left me a wreck. And you, too, though you won't admit it. It's two days to the foothills of the mountains, but we'll run off the road before we get there."

"I suppose. Very well. But we've got to be up by six. First, though, we'd better hide the carriage in that barn over there. We don't want to call something down on these people's heads in return for their hospitality."

"What do you mean?" It was the farmer speaking.

Prospero and Roger looked startled. They had been alone on the road so long that they were used to discussing their private affairs aloud. Roger got down out of the carriage and drew the farmer aside.

"Nothing will happen, I assure you, if we get that carriage out of sight before nightfall. I can't explain this thing, but if you want us to go on and not stay, we will."

"I won't hear of such a thing!" said the farmer. "I've sheltered fugitives from the kings and God knows who else. Besides, you're wizards, aren't you?"

Roger laughed and shook his head. "Maybe. Maybe. Thank you for your hospitality. Not many people are willing to take in creatures like us these days. We'll cover up the carriage later, but first I have to have a talk with my friend. Alone. We'll join you in a minute."

The farmer went into the house, and Roger went back to the carriage where Prospero was sitting.

"Listen," he said, whispering, "I think it's all right for us to stay here the night. But I keep expecting things to pounce on us when we stop. Doesn't it seem strange to you that we haven't been attacked or followed?"

"Yes, but remember how much that poor monk had to concentrate to get anything out of the book. Melichus may have given up on us. From what I can see, his work is progressing. Of course, he may be waiting for us to get to the cottage. He may—oh, let's not think about it till we have to. At any rate, I'm hungry. Let's go in and eat."

He got out of the carriage and followed Roger into the house. As they walked up the path, Roger pointed up to

˙ the bucktoothed pumpkin faces.

"If we had had one of those, we'd be traveling in a state coach."

Prospero managed a little smile. He was still thinking about the lettering in the churchyard. And he knew Roger was forcing cheerfulness.

Later, inside, the two travelers from the south sat at a smooth pine table, talking to the farmer and his wife over the ruins of a large veal-and-ham pie. It was Prospero's private and crankily repeated opinion that veal-and-ham pie was next in tastelessness to raw potatoes, but he had forgotten that opinion this evening, with the help of a sharp brown sauce made from quinces. Roger usually warned Prospero about the effect of condiments on his stomach, but tonight he kept quiet, because his friend was beginning to come out of a dangerous depression that had been on him since the bridge-wrecking incident. Part of the reason for Prospero's sudden cheerfulness was the unlikely interior of the house. The farmer, it seems, was a woodcarver, and he had filled the shelves of this long low room with scenes from local mythology: Fat saints shoved pigs through fences, elderly ladies pelted ogres with rocks, drunken kings dropped chairs out of windows onto wandering minstrels. But the best thing of all in the room was the clock over the mantel, a Nuremberg circus of cows with clacking jaws, stumbling ducks, frantically dancing angels, and waltzing bishops. In the center window over the dial was a little man who kept missing the bell with his hammer as the bell bobbed up and hit him on the head. All this, at least, is what the farmer said the clock was supposed to do. It wasn't running, and when Roger asked why, the farmer's wife pointed at the dark window.

Prospero sat there with a strange look on his face. He

got up and walked the length of the room to the fireplace, and he stood there for several minutes, toying with the jointed wooden dolls. Then, grasping the mantel, he leaned up on tiptoe and put his lips to the keyhole in the side of the clock. He whispered so softly that no one in the room heard him.

"Melichus is a fool."

Picking up the wooden crank, Prospero wound up the clock and set the pendulum swinging. The cows flapped their jaws inanely, the ducks stumbled uncertainly over the wooden platform, bishops waved their crosiers and clicked their heels, and—Prospero shoved the hands to twelve—the bewildered wooden man swung twelve times at the painted bell and missed, while the bell caught him twelve times on his shiny brass nose.

Prospero went back to his seat. "I think," he said, "that I will sleep better tonight."

The next morning, at the chilly hour of six, Prospero stood at the front door of the cottage, thanking his host, while Roger hitched up the horses and brushed hay off the carriage. The farmer had a tin box in his hand, and he was tapping it as he talked.

"I didn't think of this till morning. We—my family—have been living in this house for several hundred years, and a long way back an old man spent the night here. He did all sorts of strange things, like cleaning out a poisoned well and making the fire burn different colors. We've got all this written down. Now before he left, he gave us this key, and said that a man with the initial of P should have it. Lord knows we've had enough people here that filled that bill, even in my lifetime; Pruett, Pillion, even Pickthatch. But I have a feeling you're the one who's supposed to get it. And if you're going north to try to do something about what's happening . . ."

"I didn't say that," said Prospero. "Please don't spread rumors like that."

"I won't," said the farmer, smiling. "I wouldn't even if you had told me what you're doing. At any rate, here it is."

Prospero opened the banged-up old tin box. Inside, wrapped in a blackened rag, was a little brass key. The teeth were cut out in a cross pattern, and except for a green crust in the molded ridges of the handle, the key was shiny. There was an inscription on the barrel in squat uncial letters, but it was written in what looked like Welsh.

Prospero excitedly handed the key to Roger. "Look! You know Welsh. What does it say?"

Roger looked at it, holding it up in the bluish morning air. "Yes, it's Welsh. It says 'Gwydion of Caer Leon made me. Turn twice.' There. Does that help you?"

Prospero put the key in the buttoned inner pocket of his heavy cloak. "No," he said, "not much." He turned to the farmer. "Tell me, did the old man have a Scottish accent?"

"I wouldn't know one if I heard it, sir. My ancestors wouldn't have, either. There's no record that any of them ever left this country hereabouts, much less the North Kingdom. They wouldn't know a Scottish accent if they heard it."

"I see. Well, thank you *very* much, and if you wonder what I was doing out back, I was laying down a little spell that will make your dandelion wine the best in the country next year. And use those pentacles I drew for you. They'll keep out many things, though I doubt if they'll help with what we're all worried about."

"Good luck to you," shouted the farmer as they drove out onto the crunching gravel. Prospero leaned out of one shield-shaped door, his foot on the round black carriage step that reminded him of a musical note. He waved and shouted good-by until he could no longer see the humpy loaf of the farmhouse, and then he sat down next to Roger. For a long time he did not say anything, because he was thinking of the key in his pocket.

NINE

Anyone foolish enough to stand on Barren Tor in the booming wind of a certain wintry day in late October would have seen a box carriage scooting past below, like a black beetle. The Tor, a treeless 300-foot-high hill shaped a little like a dog's tooth, was an isolated foothill of the unnamed range of peaks that bordered the Northern Highlands. Northerners did not name mountain ranges; they were afraid that doing so would wake the spirit of the mountains, the rock-buried elemental that had once split the Mitre, a strange double peak many miles to the south. Roger and Prospero, now many days' journey from the clockmaker's cottage, had passed the Mitre a week before: It was there that they heard rumors of the War Council on the Feasting Hill. The kings were gathering, getting ready for a march on the South; they had been told by their astrologers that the fear came from the South, and so they had not destroyed the wooden bridges, as Roger thought they would; instead, they held both sides of the river with cavalry, and these men waited for the messengers from the Hill. The Southerners, no matter how well organized they were, had only fat plow horses to ride; they would be unable to prevent a march on Round-court, a city with beautiful walls of painted wood and a tiny, unreliable garrison. A quick surrender of the capital might save a lot of lives, but skirmishing and raiding could go on for a long time, and Prospero knew the temperament of certain southern rulers, who would—after the victorious north-ern kings had gone home—hold their own witch trials and take out their anger on "disloyal"—that is, weak—kings like silly old Gorm.

Meanwhile, the strange early winter threw thin rags and fingers of gray snow over the dirty, fast-decaying leaves that clotted the suddenly dry beds of streams; on the empty plain Prospero and Roger had just passed through, the snow moved in eerie swirls, falling into spirals and long lines too regular to be natural. People were terrified of the open spaces at night; in their homes they sat with blankets over their windows so that they would not see the mask of frost. Windows broke in the night, and the wind that blew through them had a voice.

On this last leg of the journey, Prospero and Roger traveled all the time, taking turns driving and sleeping as they had for weeks before they got to the farmer's house. With a candle stuck in an ashtray, Prospero sat up late, pipe in mouth, turning over pages, looking for what he knew was not there. They passed through shallow valleys where muddy pools of fog blew crazily about; long grasping fingers of it seeped through the floorboards of the carriage and thrust in at the windows. Roger raised his hand once to wave it away, and for an instant he felt something hard—the fog curled back and drifted outside again. In one shuttered hiding town a signboard screeched in a way that made the horses rear and almost tip over the carriage; Prospero raised a curtain and looked out. He was not surprised to see that the board was washed clean of any design. And now the moon began to rise into a starless sky. We who are used to the empty or rusty night skies of modern cities would not understand the fear that the people of Prospero's world felt when they saw this. They saw a haggard moon, with pinched brows and grieving mouth, rising into a blackness distant and calling. Like children lying on grass and looking into a cloud-vaulted daytime sky, they felt that they were going to fall upwards. Hollow ocean depths hung overhead, so that looking up was like standing on the edge of a cliff.

The road ran over steeper hills now; Prospero was always half surprised when an appalling height flattened out under the wheels of the carriage—from a distance it looked as though you would have to cling to the gravel with your fingers and toes. At last, though, they were in the mountains. These were not Himalayan peaks, but some of them were tall enough to thrust broken and tilting horns through frozen mats of cloud. Others were long blue ridges covered with pines. On their bristly sides you could see the zigzag lines of roads built by an ancient people no one in the north knew anything about. Whoever they were, they had dug long tunnels with decorated mouths, had built rope-lashed wooden bridges that never rotted, and had carved the mouths of rock springs into bug-eyed monsters that disturbed the dreams of travelers who came upon them at night. Prospero and Roger, looking out their wide windows at long frightening drop offs, saw a few of these vomiting horrors sticking out of dead leaf clusters or the wiry skeletons of bushes. But they seemed silly alongside the other fear.

Now Prospero had his glasses on, and he was running his finger along a line on a wrinkly map spread over both their laps.

"You see, Roger. Around the next big bend and up a road that goes through a long tunnel. There are three gates, one for wagons and two for men. There's bound to be some barrier, though, if the valley is inhabited. It's the perfect fortified place, too. The mountain is like a big tooth with a cavity. . . ."

"Charming metaphor," said Roger, feeling his jaw with his fingertips.

"Well, it is. Sheer walls and peaks that have been rounded by the wind. The bowl of grass inside must be about a mile across . . . watch out! Here's the bend."

When the carriage had rounded an upended chunk of rock that looked like the prow of a sinking boat, the carved triple entrance was there. But "some barrier" proved to be a large understatement. Each of the three wide-lipped arches was blocked by a portcullis of thick square iron bars. Behind each grate, at a distance of about twenty feet, was another grate, and so on as far as they could see in the rising coal-faced tunnels. The two men could only sit there and wonder how the black iron frames had been fitted into place, and whether they were lowered and raised by counterweights or by hand winches.

"Well," said Roger, as he got out of the carriage, "whoever they are, they're protected." He picked up a stone and threw it at the gate. It pinged and flew back at him.

"They certainly are," said Prospero, "and what is more, since I threw the tarots away, I don't believe I have the power to rip up cardboard. Destroying spells have never been much in my line anyway."

"Or mine," said Roger. He pounded his staff on the ground in frustration, threw it down, turned on his heel, and stomped off into some high bushes at the side of the road. By the way that he shoved the branches away from him, Prospero could tell that Roger was angry. He expected him to kick around in the bushes, swearing for a while, so he was surprised when Roger came back immediately with a smile on his face.

"Come here," he said. "I want you to see something."

Roger led Prospero back through the bushes—forsythia, of all things, like the ones in Prospero's back yard—and down a steep sandy path to a little lookout point. Across a small grassy valley, which was already beginning to fill with the reddish-brown mist of sunset, there was a square tower on a tall spiny pinnacle of rock. The light was bad, and even with his telescope Roger could not be sure, but it looked as though the tower was attached to the face of the mountain by a small arched bridge.

Roger was pointing excitedly. "Look, Prospero! There's our way in. Do you suppose it's a watchtower? If it is, there'll be soldiers, but if they don't have seventeen portcullises to hide behind, we may be able to get in."

Prospero borrowed the telescope and squinted. "No, it certainly doesn't look like a watchtower—at least it wasn't built for that purpose. It has four little pinnacles with knobby ornaments on them. Looks like a church tower, but where is the church that goes with it?"

"Whatever it is," said Roger, "I'd suggest that we head

for it. If it's abandoned and it isn't a way in, we can stay there the night. The carriage and horses will have to stay here, but there's some grass by the roadside. If anyone tries to steal the rig, they will go home in a squash."

"All fine and good," said Prospero, "but we are here and the tower is there. It looks about three hundred feet down to the ground, and I doubt if that boat in your bag flies."

"You might look over the edge of the cliff," said Roger.

Prospero did, and he saw stairs, wide stone slabs, some broken, some worn into cups in the middle, running back and forth down the cliff face.

"You wait here," said Roger. "I'll unhitch the horses and get the bags."

Soon they were picking their way down the steep railless stairway. Prospero's acrophobia was as bad as ever, if not worse—he kept his eyes on the rock wall and rubbed it with his shoulder, though it would have taken a concerted effort or a high wind to throw him off. At some points they found landings, wide stone platforms with parapets and stacks of boulders. These rocks, which were not too large to be lifted by strong men, had probably been put there to be dropped on the heads of pursuers. They had been there so long that they appeared to have melted into pointed humps, like piles of snowballs that were never used. When the wizards got to the bottom of the cliff, they looked across the grassy field. A light was burning high up in the tower.

As they started toward it, Prospero talked to Roger about the quietness and warmth of this mountain valley. The strange snows, the frightening sounds and sights of the plain below were not here. Twilight was drawing on, soft and deep blue, and stars could be seen overhead. It was warm for October, too—Prospero even imagined that he heard the slow finger-and-comb sound of crickets. The remark about this being, perhaps, the eye of the storm was too obvious and too frightening to be made by either of them. When they got close to the tower, they found that they were standing in the middle of jumbled stone blocks; carved and pie-faced angels stared out of bushes and ditches, and a red flaking iron cross stood upright in the middle of a wild rosebush. This was the church, destroyed by some landslide or earthquake. The tower rose straight above them on its freakish nail of rock, which was wrapped around by another stair, this one railed for a change.

"This is all very convenient," said Prospero, looking up at the long lighted window. "I hope we are not going to be the guests of some ogre."

"We shall see," said Roger. And they started up.

At the top of the stairs they saw an open arched door, and in front of it stood a blond-bearded monk. He was holding a metal basket of fire on a wooden stick, and when they reached the last few steep steps, he stuck the torch in the wall and helped them up.

"Greetings," he said. "Welcome to the Green Oratory. I'm here by myself, and I'm probably the only monk for miles."

"I wouldn't be so sure," said Roger. He tipped his hat and showed the bald spot on his red-fringed head. "What are you doing up *here*?"

"I grow plants," said the monk. "And I do things with them. Come in and let me show you around."

The guided tour of the Green Oratory showed that the monk indeed grew plants: lime trees in tubs, frazzled cacti in barrels, jack-in-the-pulpits in pots, and Venus's-flytraps in cages. He had built flooring to divide the bell tower into rooms; they were connected by ladders, but Prospero's fear of heights extended to fear of straight-up ladders, so he went up the dumb-waiter with the luggage. When they came to the top of the belfry, there were the bells, dirty and pigeon-streaked, but they had been turned upside down and filled with dirt. Vines and creepers with purple leaves and red waxy droplet flowers dripped over their sides. The monk would not tell Prospero and Roger how he kept the steamy atmosphere of an arboretum in this cold stone building, but he did enjoy exchanging plant information with Prospero.

Now they were on the roof, where all sorts of night-blooming flowers opened bells, trumpets, and puffy Chinese-lantern mouths. The roof of the tower was covered with a burgundy-colored moss that Prospero had never seen before. Roger was smiling and shaking his head while the monk walked around, fingering leaves and talking proudly of his collection. Prospero finally had to interrupt him.

"Please. All this is lovely, but we've got to get to the village beyond this mountain. Is there any way in?"

The monk looked unhappy. "I saw you coming down the stairs on the other side, so I guess you know about those gates. The villagers chased me out a couple of months ago when I was picking mushrooms at night. They have plants up there that you wouldn't believe. Why . . . oh yes. No, that's the only way up. But why go there? It's really not a very friendly place these days."

"I can't explain," said Prospero, thinking wearily of all the people to whom he had said "I can't explain," "but we've got to get in. Haven't you been wondering why it's still al-most like summer up here in this valley? And haven't you heard what's happening down below?"

The monk pointed to a little white dovecote in the

corner. "I've heard, all right—from them—and I hope I can ride it out. I don't know much magic except plant magic, but I *can* tell you that this is not a healthy place now. It's close and muggy down in that valley there at night. Come over to the edge and look down."

Prospero and Roger saw a blue mist floating below—it was like water, and like water it distorted shapes. Broken rocks looked wavy, and tall stalks bent sharply at the top. Long grass was rippling like weeds at the bottom of a stream.

"It all looks as though it might blow away in a minute," said the monk. "When I'm down there at night I don't feel real at all."

"I've seen worse than that down on the plain," said

Prospero. "And we may be able to stop all this, God knows how. Isn't there *any* way up? Think!"

The monk walked around, pounding his fist in his hand. He kicked a tin watering can across the roof.

"Way up. Way up. Say! No, that's ridiculous. Still . . . wait here a minute."

He went down through the trap door, and made a lot of noise in the room below. When he came back up he was carrying two pots, and in each one was an ordinary-looking creeper vine.

"This," he said, "is Sensitive Anaconda."

"It looks like Creeping Charlie to me," said Prospero, who had such a plant in his front parlor.

The monk looked hurt. "Well, it isn't. And it may get you over that wall. Follow me, and may I request silence?"

Prospero and Roger followed the monk, who solemnly carried the plants, one in each hand, across the little wooden bridge that connected the tower with the mountain. On the other side was a narrow rock shelf and beyond it was a dank-smelling mushroom cave. The procession stopped at the mouth of the cave, and the monk set the plants down. He looked up at the slightly furrowed granite wall that rose at least a hundred feet above the shelf; it was not only perpendicular, it actually seemed to lean out a bit at the top. Now he began to conjure, and his style was odd. He stood with his hand over his face, muttering, as if he were trying to remember the answer to a hard question. As he talked, the plants rose, swaying like charmed snakes. They dug green tendrils into the smooth rock, making cracks where they did not find them. Up they went, wriggling and twisting, until the tops of the two vines were out of sight. The monk waited, tapping his foot. Suddenly the vines tightened, vibrating like plucked strings. They had caught hold of some rocks at the top.

Prospero looked pale. "Excuse me," he said, "but I'm not very good at climbing. I get dizzy in the lower limbs of apple trees."

"Well, lucky man that you are, you won't have to climb," said the monk. "Hold this."

He put a pot in each man's hand. The vines, imitating the corkscrew motion that the monk now made with his finger, wrapped themselves tightly around the wizards, several times around. He gave each man his bag and staff.

"And so farewell," he said. "Come back and tell me what this was all about."

The vines began to wrap more and more lengths of green cable around the two somewhat alarmed men, who now started to rise, slowly and solemnly. Prospero thought for a second of what would happen if this eccentric plant grower was one of Melichus' helpers, or, God forbid, Melichus himself. But he shrugged his shoulders as well as he could with six bands of vine around him and tightened his grip on the carpetbag. There was no way up but this, and up they went, scraping their backs on hard rock. The monk, who was waving his watering can at them, got smaller and smaller in the moonlight.

By the time they got to the top of the mountain wall, each now had a fat green rubber tire around him. But when they were safe on the broad rock rim, the vines loosened and slithered back down the sheer face. Like someone preparing to go on stage, Prospero stood with his back to the little valley, squared his shoulders, brushed back his hair, and shook granite dust off his sleeves. Finally, he took a deep breath, let it out, and turned around.

The valley below him, gray in the rising moon, was a wide hilly basin of close-cropped grass, dotted with clover. Dark wrinkled rocks stuck out of folds in the ground. Houses, squatty loaf shapes with thatched mops, ran in even rows over the one long central ridge. He counted them—one . . . two . . . hmmm . . . twenty. Where was the cottage he had stayed in? It must be in the shadows at the back of the valley, up under those four upright slabs of stone. Then he turned and saw Roger.

Roger stood listening. His arms were raised to fend off something, and he was staring in fear at the pleasant little town, as if it were about to fly at him in a hail of boards and stone. Finally he lowered his arms, wiped his face, and turned to Prospero. His voice showed that he was breathing heavily.

"You . . . you know, all the way up here I thought to myself, 'What if we are going to the wrong place? What if we are leaving the field of battle, where we ought to meet Melichus and try to beat him?' I don't think that now. There's something here, all right, and it doesn't like us. We are going to have a hard time getting out of this place."

Prospero looked around him. "I don't feel anything. That may be a bad sign, because this fight is mainly between Melichus and me. Maybe I'm not meant to notice anything—yet."

"Well, come on," said Roger. "Let's see what's down here. We may as well give up all hope of sneaking up to the cottage unnoticed. If they can't see two men silhouetted in moonlight on the edge of a cliff, they won't see us if we walk through the middle of their town."

They stumbled down the long slope of loose and broken stones that led to the edge of the sweet-smelling clover field.

The houses in the distance had looked dark from above, and now they looked just as dark.

"This is strange," said Prospero. "It's only eight o'clock at night, and even in a little farming town there'd be *one* light. And look! The shutters are closed."

"Yes. They really have a wild life up here."

Prospero and Roger walked on, listening for some sound, some barking dog or screeching nightwalking cat. When they reached the little town the houses seemed more than dark—they were empty, abandoned, and dead. Blackness lay in the cracks of the broken shutters, and in the spaces between doors and sills. Prospero walked up to one silent cottage and rapped several times on the door. He heard nothing, but as he stood waiting, his hand passed near the keyhole. A cold draft, so cold that it stung his palm, was blowing from inside the house.

He turned and walked back to Roger, who was looking around him with more and more apprehension.

"Roger, this is more than very strange. Didn't that silly monk say there were people up here who threw him out?"

"Yes, he did. But they may not have been people."

"Let's go on."

A little farther ahead—nothing was very far from anything else in this tiny town—was the market place, a square plot overgrown with weedy grass and withered dandelion stems. In the middle was a fountain with a low carved curb. Fountains were common enough in market places, but this one was quite elaborate. The sides of the round basin were carved into several bas-relief panels, and in the center was the figure of a hooded man reading. Unfortunately the fountain was not running, and the basin was full of dirt. And flowers. Very odd-looking flowers.

Prospero sat on the smooth worn lip of the basin and tweaked a leaf with his finger.

"These *are* strange flowers. You remember what the monk said, Roger. He said they had flowers up here you wouldn't—"

Roger suddenly leaped forward, grabbed Prospero's hand, and jerked him away, so violently that the two of them fell in a heap on the ground, amid many shouts and what-the-devils, all of them from Prospero. He picked himself up and stared at Roger, who was himself staring intently at the fountain.

"Now what in God's name . . ."

"The flowers. You didn't see the monk's drawings, but I did."

"The monk? The one down there with the plants? Why —oh! *Oh!* Good Lord, the plants in the book!"

"Yes. And let us now have a look at those carved panels, if we dare." Roger's voice was shaking.

The panels, to neither man's surprise, were familiar: the Witch of Endor, the silhouetted figure in the terrible black window. What the other pictures were they never found out, for as Prospero was straightening up after looking at the first two, he saw a candle burning in a window down the street on the right.

"Look."

"Yes. I see it and I want to run. But we must go to it."

"At this point, anything else would be insane, don't you think?"

Roger agreed, and they slowly started to walk toward the little haloed light. It was shining in the front window of a stone house that was a little larger than the two on either side of it. Its roof was of slate and the shingles looked newly laid. For whatever good it would do them, Prospero and Roger stayed close to the shadowed walls and eaves of the nearer house as they edged down the lane. Finally they were at the corner of the large house, and they flattened themselves against the rough stuccoed wall. Prospero was the first to reach the window, and, much against his better judgment and the shouting of his instincts, he looked.

What he saw was an old white-maned man, his back to the window. He was seated at a polished table and he was reading a book. A single candle in a pewter stand dribbled wax on the dark varnished surface. Nearby on the table lay a half loaf of bread from which a piece had been roughly torn, and there was a tin cup that might have had wine in it.

In the few seconds that Prospero stood there looking, he felt terribly afraid. He imagined that the faint steam from his breath on the pane would catch the old man's eye. But the reading figure did not move. Prospero edged back, and Roger squeezed past him to look. A couple of seconds later they were both on all fours, crawling back to the alley between the two houses. They whispered excitedly.

"To think he is up here!" said Roger. "But it does make sense, in a way. Do you think he knows we're here?"

"No," said Prospero, crossing himself. "If you want my opinion, I think that hell could gape and not tear him away from that cursed book. He's caught, but then maybe we are too."

"At least we know why he stopped chasing us," said Roger. "Which way is your cottage? Do you have any idea of which way it is?"

"North," said Prospero, pointing up the dark valley. "I think we had better go on hands and knees till we get out of this lane. And then run like the devil for the back of the valley! Follow me."

The two men crept along slowly, lifting their satchels and setting them down softly a few feet in front of them. And when they were in the open, behind the houses, they ran, but nothing followed them from that dark house.

The shadows of the four monoliths rose higher over them as they ran. Roger tripped on a stone and almost fell.

"Where is it? Maybe he's torn it down."

"No . . . no, there it is! Just a little farther."

There it was, a narrow wooden house with Gothic pointed windows and a steep roof. As they got closer, Roger could tell that this had been mainly Prospero's work, not Melichus'. The posts that held up the sagging porch roof were carved into beanstalks, and a few traces of the original yellow paint could be seen in the cracks. Knobby white wooden icicles dripped from the eaves, and the deep-paneled front door had an oval stained-glass inset. Up on the creaky porch, the two wizards set down their bags and stared a minute at the dark jeweled glass. Roger lit a match.

"Do you suppose that key the farmer gave you fits this lock?"

"No," said Prospero, who was rummaging in the inside pocket of his winter cloak. "I have carried the key to this door with me for years. When I'm looking for the key to the root cellar or the linen closet, I always come across the thing and wonder why I keep it."

He pulled out a small iron ring full of different-size keys. Selecting a big one with a quatrefoiled handle, he placed it in the cherub-mouth of the lockplate. The door rattled open. Roger shut it after them and lit another match, and they saw the shadowy outline of a few small wooden chairs. An empty copper candlestick stood nearby on a dusty table, and Prospero stuck a lighted candle—his last one—in it.

"Well, here we are," he said. "Now if I can only remember where I put that globe."

"If it's still here," said Roger. "Look at the floor."

The dusty gray boards in front of them were covered with long narrow footprints. Prospero stood looking at them. He bit his lip several times until it hurt, and he started nervously clenching and unclenching his fists.

"It was to be expected. But he *can't* take it away." His voice dropped. "At least, I think he can't. Come on. I remember where I put it, and I was the last one out."

He grabbed the candlestick and led Roger to a corner cupboard at the back of the cottage's one large room. The round-topped door stood on a little waist-high sill, and its knob, a piece of blue-streaked porcelain, was startlingly cold to the touch. While Roger held the candle, Prospero opened the cupboard. Inside he could see stacks of bowls and plates, last used—as far as he knew—by Melichus himself. On a separate shelf, over the others, was the green-glass paperweight. He was almost afraid to touch it, and he reached for it twice, pulling his hand away each time. Finally he closed his fingers on it—it was colder than the knob had been—and he lowered it carefully. Roger saw that he was covering it with his hand.

"Let's light more candles," said Prospero. "I don't want to look at this strange little thing in the dark."

He set the green object on a table and, with Roger, searched about until they found a bundle of candles on the mantelpiece, tied up with some rotted string. They spent several minutes sticking them in wall sconces and dishes all around the room, then lit them all. Prospero was still not satisfied, and besides he wanted an excuse to keep him from looking at the magic globes. So he decided to build a fire. The logs that he and Melichus had left there so long before lay near the fireplace, soft honeycombs of mushy sawdust. He kicked one and a swarm of beetles crawled out, scurrying away to find cracks in the floor. But another log pile lay nearby, further evidence that someone had been there recently. Roger knelt in front of the black sooty-smelling hearth, laid a small fire, and struck several matches before he could get the pile of twigs to light. Prospero was pacing up and down, looking at the door.

"The globes aren't dusty either," he said. "And there were marks of hands scrabbling in the dust on the shelf. What do you think? I'm afraid."

"So am I," said Roger, who was pumping the fire with a cracked old leather bellows. "So am I."

He straightened up. The fire was crackling and throwing long jumping shadows on the opposite wall.

"Well, that's that. Now let's look at that thing on the table. Prospero! For heaven's sake, stop pacing!"

"Oh, very well. I'd feel better if he'd just burst in on us. But he's not going to. Let's see what the globes are doing."

They pulled two chairs up to the round oak table where the glass pyramid sat sparkling between two candles, like some strange shrine. At first the globes were empty and transparent. A few bubbles frozen inside them made specks in the green water-shadow that floated on the table. Then, slowly, the three lower spheres began to form a picture. There was the crossroads, there were the high banks, the bare trees, the leaning stone marker, and the softly falling snow. Prospero pulled the paperweight closer and stared hard at the uppermost globe. From the pinpoint bubbles, rounded images expanded till their bowed and distorted shapes filled the whole ball, and then they burst to let new images form. All these pictures were familiar to Prospero: his bookcase, a hatrack, a bust of some Roman dignitary. Finally, after much swirling, the ball focused on a single scene: Prospero's house, seen from the front lawn. The porch was piled with leaves, the shades were drawn as Prospero had left them, and long bands of that uncanny snow lay in curving ridges around the house. With an effort, Prospero brought the house closer, till he could see the square window in the front door. It was covered with the frost-mask, two running empty eyes, and a long howling mouth. He tried to get close enough to look in the window, but the empty face filled the glass and burst. The ball was clear and green again.

"Now," said Prospero, "I'm going to speak to Melichus."

Roger jumped up and put a hand on his arm. "No, don't! You don't know what will happen if you meet face to face."

"That's right, I don't. But we can't just sit here fiddling with this ball while he scares the world to death or destroys it. He may not know we're here, but he will soon. Anything after that is up to him."

Roger sat down and folded his arms. "Very well. You make about as much sense as anything does right now. But if you need my help, just grab my hand."

"All right. But relax. This may take quite some time. Melichus isn't something I own or someplace I've been. He can resist if he wants to. And he *will* want to. In fact, this globe may be the only way to reach him."

Prospero put both hands on the glass and stared at it. Slowly it began to fill with a flat blue ink, till the whole ball was blanked out. This was all that happened. For a full half hour Prospero squeezed the ball, hammered it on the table, spoke to it, made signs over it. Nothing happened. At last he stood up with the thing clenched in his hand. The sweat on his face shone in the firelight.

"Melichus! I call on you by the secret name you were given by Michael Scott. That is . . ."

He spoke the name and the room grew darker. One candlestick fell over and the others burned blue. The flames in the fireplace leaped up the flue with a shriek, leaving the half-burned logs suddenly gray and cold. In the dark chilly room the two men bent over the glass ball. It seemed to be coming apart. The glass remained intact, but the blackness

inside split along a jagged line, like an egg, opening to a burning white center. The light hurt Prospero's eyes and he turned away, but when he looked again the light was gray and sullen, like a winter afternoon. He saw an old man whose dirty red eyes were sunk in wrinkled hollow caves. The thin white lips were parted and the yellow teeth were set on edge. His hand held the trembling page of a book, and Prospero could see that it was the last page. The stare that met his was not one of knowing hatred, scorn, or bitter triumph. It was much more frightening than that. What Prospero saw was the blank angry glare of an animal that has been interrupted at its meal. He could not even tell if Melichus recognized him. The two rheumy eyes focused on his for a second, and then they seemed to be looking past him. Prospero relaxed for a second, and the two halves of the egg slammed together with a boom that made him drop the glass on the floor. It did not break, but a crooked line of white was etched into the outer surface of the globe.

Prospero stood there a long time, looking down at the scarred globe. The candles were burning brightly again, and a stiff wind was rattling the front windows of the house. Finally he bent over, picked the thing up, and put it back on the table. Now, as Roger sat staring at him in amazement, he began to walk around the room, touching things, looking under chairs, running his finger over dusty panes.

"Hah! I thought so! He's crazier than I thought!"

"What do you mean?"

"He's put it all back. The way it was. Look. We know Melichus was here—it could hardly have been anyone else. And the marks in the dust show that he moved things around, that he probably took the globe off the shelf and looked at it. Well, before he left he put everything back the way it was when I left. When we first lit candles and I could see the way the room looked, I thought 'It's all the same, every bit of it!' You see that book over there on the edge of the chair?"

"Yes."

"Well, when I left here Lord knows how many years ago I stood at the door with a book in my hand. I even remember the title, *Roman Divination*. I was wondering whether or not I wanted it. I decided that I didn't, so I threw it onto that chair over there. It skidded to the edge and almost fell off. It's still there, hanging on the edge, though the dust marks show it has been picked up recently. Now, either Melichus has gotten fanatically meticulous in his old age, or this is a circle he doesn't want disturbed."

"What about the new pile of firewood?"

"That's *new*, but all the old things were put back. He must have found that it felt very wrong for things to be out of place. Now, as I say, it might have been just fussiness. But let's see."

Moving around the room in quick jumps and darts, Prospero started upsetting things. First he tipped over the table—the paperweight hit the floor and skidded into a corner. Then he pitched the book into the fireplace, smashed a chair against a wall, and finally, grandiosely, he swept his arm along the mantel—dishes, candles, bottles, and cups fell and flew up in a splintering dusty cascade. He stopped, panting, in the middle of the room.

"There! Now if *that* doesn't stir him from his bibliophilic torpor, then . . ."

"For God's sake! Look!"

Roger was pointing at the door. The stained glass oval, a beautiful flower design in cobalt blue and deep crimson, was shining, as though someone had thrown a light on it from the outside. And on the wall opposite the door a watery light pattern appeared. It was full of skeletal winding shadows, and it formed, like the frost patterns, a distorted blank face. The long mouth moved and a harsh, flat, angry voice spoke.

"Put it back. Put back the globes."

Prospero stood there in the middle of the room, and in the ghastly light the face threw on everything, his own face looked corpselike and frozen. He swallowed hard, and all the ridged muscles in his face and throat convulsed.

"No. I will not."

The voice began to speak again, this time in a high, almost hysterical chant. The words were ugly and strange, but Prospero knew their meaning. The dusty air of the dark old room was full of this rising and falling sound. Prospero raised his arm, pointed at the trembling blotch of light, and spoke a single word that shook his whole body. The door slammed open and a cold earth-smelling wind blew in. The face spread into a mottled screen that covered the whole wall, writhed, shot halfway across the ceiling, and then slowly began to draw together again, into a tighter, more recognizable, and more brightly shining mask. Roger leaped up and struck at the wall with his staff—it bounced out of his hand and flew across the room. His arm was numb to the elbow and he found that he could not move. The chant went on, rising. Prospero turned and started to stumble slowly toward the table, moving his arms like someone struggling in water. He got to the far corner of the room, stooped, picked up the glass object that was now totally black in all its globes, and started for the door, moving his free arm in front of him, as if he were clearing something away. He stopped and turned in the black doorway. His face was very pale but he was smiling.

"Good-by, Roger. I hope we meet again." And then, to the face, which was shaking like the light of a lantern in someone's trembling fist: "If you want this, *come and get it.*"

He reeled out onto the porch. The face flew apart into wild jabs and streaks of light that shot all over the room. Roger suddenly found that he could move again, and he rushed to the door and looked down the moonlit path. Prospero was running with his cloak bundled tightly around him, and halfway down the road he simply disappeared.

TEN

At first Prospero felt that he was inside one of the green-glass globes. Everything looked the way it does when you hold a piece of colored cellophane up in front of your eyes, except that it was all rounded, bowed outward—things in the distance diminished into tiny curved perspectives. Then the walls of the globe spread outward, farther, farther, and the green faded to the cold dark of a winter night. He was standing at the crossroads. There were the high banks, made higher by long white drifts; there were the bare black trees, and overhead the branches of a huge oak creaked under piles of wet snow. But there was no stone marker. Prospero was standing where it should have been, on a little triangular patch of raised ground. A white light lay all around him, and when he looked up into the thick, wet, slowly falling flakes he saw a swaying lamp overhead, a bare electric bulb with a fluted porcelain reflector. It hung from a long black wire.

He stood there with the green paperweight in his hand, looking up at the frigid, dazzlingly cold light. He felt empty, drained, and he knew that he had no magic power left. His bag and staff were back at the cottage with Roger, not that they would be any help to him now. He couldn't charm a single snowflake out of the air. Was this his punishment? And was he exiled to some place that existed only in the world of those globes, while Melichus was free to finish what he had started?

The snow fell quietly, settling on his shoulders in wet sticky patches. And as it got darker, he began to get the feeling that he dreaded. Someone was coming up the road on his left. He could not see anything there. Outside the cold, slowly swaying circle of lamplight, the road ran off into a tangle of skeletal trees. But someone was coming, Melichus was coming for him. Now, far down the road, he could see a tiny yellow point of light, bobbing. Wrapping his woolen cloak around him and turning up his collar—the snowflakes were icy on his neck—he started to run in the other direction. The snow had packed down into a slick smooth track under the loose sparkling flakes—he fell down, got up, skidded, and fell down again, his hands sinking into the stinging cold. He crawled on his hands and knees to the sunken shoulder of the road and found that he could walk in the drifts. Frozen grass crunched under him, and the wind began to blow in his face. Dots of snow rushed at him out of the darkness, and he had to keep wiping his eyes as he staggered along.

He kept walking, as fast as he could, for what must have been several miles. Sometimes he fell into a hole filled with rotten leaves or scraped his leg on a snow-covered post, but he kept going. Every now and then he looked behind him, and the moving light was still there. Once a car came around a bend, a boxy black shape crawling slowly behind two frosted moons of light, but he hid in the ditch until it was gone. He doubted that they could or would help anyone who looked the way he did, and for some reason he did not want to meet any of the people in this world, not just yet. If there was a way out of all this, he felt that he would have to find it himself. But the light was getting nearer.

At the top of a low hill, under a huge chestnut tree that dropped shovelfuls of snow on him as he stood looking around uncertainly, Prospero stopped to rest. He saw that he was standing under a stone wall, and that there was a little flight of stairs nearby; it was merely a soft bumpy incline in all this snow, but maybe he could climb it. As he made his way toward it, he noticed a large flat wooden sign propped against one of the ball-topped gateposts. He brushed away the snow with a stinging reddened hand, struck a match, and read:

M. MILLHORN
LAWNMOWERS & AXES SHARPENED
HAMMER HANDLES MADE
USED NAILS AND BACK DOORS FOR SALE

Prospero rubbed more snow away from the bottom of the sign and looked again. That was what it said, all right. He tried to laugh, but it came out as a phlegmy cough.

"Well, M. Millhorn, you sound interesting. Here we come."

Prospero kicked some footholds in the snow that covered the steps, and he slowly climbed up, plunging his hands into the snow in front of him to steady himself. At the top, he stood up in the knee-high snow and stared into the swirling dark. There behind a couple of skinny pines was a big square farmhouse with deep-set corniced windows and a scalloped rooftree. A light was on downstairs, but the yellow shades, patched with colored pieces of newspaper, were drawn. He kicked his way through the snow, making long scars in the wet drifts. From this height he had a good view of the road, and when he looked, he saw, far down the row of fence posts, the light. It stopped, dropped to a lower position, then rose and went slowly swinging along, as if the bearer had stopped to look for footprints. They wouldn't be hard to find, Prospero thought, and he kicked harder at the packed snow in front of him.

Moving at this spread-legged awkward gait, he took a long time, or what seemed a long time, to reach the front steps. Up on the narrow front stoop, he banged with a numb fist on the yellow door. Thumping and bumping inside, and a sound like someone upsetting a keg of nails. Finally the door opened, and there in the harsh glare of a single bulb that hung from a long knotted cord was a small man in a square-cut beard. He wore oval rimless spectacles and a black skullcap, and over his shoulders was a black silk shawl with elaborate gold tassels. His striped floor-length robe, something between a dressing gown and a cassock, might once have been brown and blue. He looked Prospero up and down and laughed silently.

"Well, come on in. You'll catch your death out there."

Prospero thanked him and stepped in the door, brushing snow off his cloak as he went. The room was an incredible mess: cracked chamber pots, upended sewing machines, fat-lipped spittoons, iron-wheeled lawn mowers, ax handles stacked like rifles, fussy-fringed floor lamps with green-marble insets, an isinglass-windowed stove with a brass vase on top, and several kegs of bent nails, one of them tipped over. On the wall was a crazy collection of picture frames, some with dark pictures in them. One of them showed several dogs with pipes in their mouths. They were sitting around a table playing poker.

The little man stood looking at Prospero for a couple of seconds, and then he turned sharply and went to the window. Raising the dirty shade a couple of inches, he looked out.

"From what I can see," he said, "you don't have much time. You'd better do what I tell you."

Prospero gaped. He felt an urge to run around the room touching things.

"Are you real? Is this house real?"

The man laughed quietly with his tongue between his teeth.

"Well, these days you can't tell. Yes, I'm real. A damn sight more real than you are, if you catch my meaning. Well, let's get going. I've been waiting for this for a long time."

He went to a high glazed bookcase full of vellum-backed volumes; from where he stood Prospero could read titles like *Aristotelis Opera* and *Mysterium Cosmographicum*. Standing on a cane-bottomed chair, the man lifted down from the top of the case a huge untitled tome with the Seal of Solomon stamped on the side. He lugged it over to a large wooden lectern and opened it. It was full of black, shaded Hebrew characters.

Prospero knew what it was and he looked with awe at the man, who was unconcernedly thumbing through the book.

"The Kabbala?" Prospero asked.

"The Kabbala. Now hurry downstairs and find the door you want. When I say 'Back doors for sale' that's what I mean."

"But can I pay you? What can I do? You don't know how grateful I am . . ."

"Yes I do. For payment, though, I'll take this little glass doodad. It can't be worth much, but it'll look nice on the mantel."

Prospero looked at him and the little man looked back, smiling quietly. But at that moment the front door banged open and a rush of cold wind blew a thin line of snow skittering across the floor. Outside, at the bottom of the snowy steps, they could see the light of a single square lantern.

The man talked fast and nervously now. "Give me that thing, for God's sake! You can't help me now, and you can't take it back with you. One way or another, I'll keep him from getting it, so get on with you! *Go!*"

Prospero looked at the yellow light that hung in a fog of snowflakes, at the man in the black skullcap who held out his hand, and he gave him the paperweight. He turned to go, but with his hand on the knob of the cellar door, he turned and looked. The man was dragging the lectern over in front of the door.

Now Prospero was clumping down the thin slats of the cellar stairs. Leaning against the wall opposite him was a row of doors: big paneled doors with peeling black paint, ivory colored doors with broken star-frosted panes, a door covered with speckled brown leather and pyramid-headed nails. The line stretched away into the coal-smelling dark basement, and Prospero walked along it, pulling doors toward him and looking behind them: nothing but rough mortared stones. Overhead a mournful winding high-pitched chant started, but it was cut off by an incredibly angry word.

A long flash of blue light shot down the cellar stairs—Prospero, several yards away, could feel the heat of it. Doors, doors, doors. For a minute he had the horrible fear that he would see the two of them coming down the stairs after him. Then he stopped short. In front of him was a little pointed door that looked like a tombstone. A dirty yellow card was stuck to it with a red thumbtack. The card said "Root Cellar."

There was no doorknob, of course, so Prospero tried the opening spell. Nothing happened. Overhead the war between the wandering chant and the loud bursting voice went on. The cobwebbed ceiling shook, bits of dirt sifted down from the shaking and grinding rafters, and a chamber pot flew down the stairs. It smashed on the wall with a loud pop, like a huge light bulb. Prospero stood looking at the door, his arms at his sides. Then, suddenly, he smiled and laughed, shaking his head. He grabbed the door with both hands and lifted it toward him. It was not fastened to anything and came away from the wall easily. Behind it was a long tunnel and a slippery-looking rock incline. Carrying the door in front of him like a shield, he backed into the tunnel, setting down the heavy wooden slab when it was—he hoped—back in place. He could not hear the noises overhead any more.

Prospero took one step in the darkness and fell down. He slid and kept on sliding, on wet chunky stones that bit into his back as he fell. It was not a steep incline, but there was no way of stopping, and by the time he got to the bottom he was shaken, nauseated, and bruised. He looked around and saw that he was in a forest that looked familiar, if ordinary elms, oaks, and maples can look familiar. It was the forest behind his house.

Now he was running down a path he had walked along many times on quiet afternoons in the late slanting light.

The owls of his nightmare appeared overhead and swooped down on him, great hissing moon-eyed bags of dusty feathers. He swung at one and it ripped open, emptying on him a cloud of green buzzing insects. They clung to his face and bit, brushing his eyelids with rustling wings. He ran on with his eyes closed, waving his arms, and suddenly the bugs dropped off him, dead. He was in his back yard.

Everything looked the way it had in the magic glass: the lines of snow, the frost on the windows. He saw that the fountain was not running. A long muddy streak ran down the satyr's sides and the marble basin was full of caked smelly earth. Two dead birds lay in it. The apple tree was covered with dead rattling leaves and small wrinkled mushy brown stones. Everything lay under a dull gray light; the bulging clouds overhead looked as though they were going to burst. But every object in the yard threw a shadow, a small dark trembling patch. One of them, cast by nothing that Prospero could see, lay on the grass near him. It started to crawl toward him slowly.

He shoved his way through the bare forsythia branches and reached the back door, his key already in his hand. The lock turned, the door opened, he was inside. And when he slammed the door behind him he could feel something rushing back into place. The house was under siege.

Prospero went about lighting candles in the musty dark; they burned with a pale gassy glare and sometimes guttered out in a wind that was not blowing. Outside, behind the staring faces, the heavy dark waited. Now and then, as he went about the house examining the rooms, he put his hand on an outside wall and imagined that he felt it straining inward. The plaster was covered with wandering thready cracks.

He went to the living room and pulled down magic books, one after the other, trying spells. Nothing worked. When he had tried about ten books he threw the pile on the floor in the middle of the room, grabbed a Florence flask that had something brown crusted inside it, and smashed it in the fireplace. He went upstairs.

In the glass-walled observatory he picked up instruments and stared at them. The metal barometers were stuck on "Storm" and the liquid was high up in the Torricellian tube. Prospero stood there idly wondering how there could be low pressure when the whole house seemed about to cave inward. And then he started to think about what he could do. Nothing. He took off his glasses, rubbed his eyes, put the glasses on again, and sat on the edge of a desk, looking out over the dead landscape.

He had been staring for some minutes when the clouds began to move very strangely. They came apart in places, in stringy rips and seams, like torn cloth. The sky that showed behind was dark red, and the garish light spattered on tree-tops. Now the clouds were rushing about and heaving, shooting jabs of that bloody light in all directions. The shadows below contracted to pinpoints and shot suddenly out into acre-wide blots. Across the road that ran toward Brakespeare the ground opened, a huge saliva-strung mouth, and out of it crawled shapes with arms and legs. And now thunder, or something like thunder—heavy, flat, ear-pressing booms without reverberations, each one louder than the next. In the crazy jumping red light Prospero fell to the floor, his hands on his ears. Almost hysterically he was thinking the same thing over and over: "What can I do? What can I do? What—"

The key. Gwydion of Caer Leon's key. It was still in his

inner pocket. Now, what to use it on? He had a key for every bureau drawer and cupboard in the house, except . . . of course! Prospero got up and started down the steps, as the booming and flashing went on. The floor and walls seemed uncertain, as though they might not be there the next minute. He had the horrible feeling that needles and nails were about to shoot into his feet when he stepped forward, and he had to force himself to put one foot after another on the winding stairs, which were now bending and giving like the melting steps of the inn at Five Dials.

Halfway down from the observatory, in the paneled wall of the corkscrew staircase, was a little locked cubbyhole. Prospero had never known what it was for, and he had tried many times to pry it open. Now he had the key, and in it went, turning around twice. The little door popped open, and inside, in the rushing and retreating red light that was beating at the observatory windows, he saw a small carved squirrel with a note in its two buck teeth. The note said:

USE THE SPELL, FOOL.

"Spell?" shouted Prospero, throwing the squirrel down the stairs. "What spell?"

Then he knew. Down the stairs, rushing and stumbling, taking them two at a time. In the living room he plowed through the books on the floor till he found the duplicate of the one he had put in his bag, the one that was God knows where now. In a loud splintery ripping of wood, a rising roaring of wind, in a cloud of plaster dust shooting down from the ceiling, and as the front door flew open and something Prospero refused to look at stepped in, he shouted the square-noted spell that had never been good for anything. The clocks, run down and clogged with dust, started to strike, at first wheezily, then in rapid *pings* and *booms* and *whangs* and *wauwauwaus;* the brass kettles hanging on hooks over the kitchen stove boomed together. All this noise, amazingly, sounded over the flat thuds, which now grew softer and then trailed away like ordinary summer thunder. The front door, in which no figure stood, banged gently in a wet-smelling breeze, and the light that threw its long, slanting dusty rays in at Prospero's wet dripping windows was the light of four o'clock on a bright October afternoon.

ELEVEN

On Christmas Eve a screeching ice storm swept through the countryside around Brakespeare, and the next afternoon the trees of Prospero's forest jingled and flashed like chandeliers in the light of a small cold sun. In the back yard the mayor, his chain of office hanging over one arm like a priest's maniple, was trying out his new pearl-and-ivory inlaid crossbow on some red-feathered popinjays that swayed on the tops of tall wooden poles. He was not having much luck, since in the course of the previous three-day party he had found Prospero's stock of carnation brandy. In the living room the innkeeper of the Running Hog and Emperor's Elbow was mixing a slate-colored drink called Bishop's Disgust in a beer barrel that had been full the day before. King Gorm, dressed in a white cassock with a powder-blue cummerbund, sat in a corner reading the *Krankenhammer*. Villagers hefting double-handled beer mugs occasionally stopped in front of him and bowed uncertainly. In a back room the plant-raising monk looked like a cartoonist's Laocoön, because he was trying to break up a fight between his Sensitive Anaconda and Prospero's Creeping Charlie. On the cupola of the observatory the hippopotamus, painted a tasteful red and green, huffed out an asthmatic "We Three Kings."

Prospero and Roger were in the back yard with the mayor, and they were throwing snowballs at the thickly glazed satyr, whose ears sprouted huge ice trumpets. Roger had arrived in mid-November, driving the black box carriage; he brought with him the plant monk, Prospero's bag and staff, and enough stories about what had happened to him up north to fill all the evenings before Christmas. Prospero's powers had returned. When he grew tired of throwing snowballs he ran around the yard touching the forsythia bushes, which burst crackling from their ice shells, shot forth pasty yellow flowers, and quacked out the shawm music Josquin des Prés had composed for the coronation of Louis XII.

Finally, toward evening, everyone went home, even the mayor, who had stripped the gears on his crossbow's windlass. Prospero stood at the snow-rounded front gate wishing the Lord Mayor a Merry Christmas, while Roger swept broken bottles and things past the sleeping Gorm, who was staying the night whether he knew it or not. Suddenly, from an upstairs window, came a horrible retching sound. Only the mirror could make such noises at such a volume. Prospero looked quickly at the lighted bedroom window, and turned to the mayor.

"You'll have to excuse me, sir, but I think something's wrong upstairs. It's the mirror."

The mayor stared at him sluggishly from brandied eye-balls. "Do mirrors drink?"

"Some do. Here, take this bottle, there's a little left. Good-by again and Merry Christmas."

Prospero rushed inside and, with an amused glance at the snoring Gorm, ran upstairs. The mirror's cranky voice could be heard all over the house.

"*Akkkk! Hcchh-ptui-phoo!* Well, how would you like it if people came traipsing across *your* tongue all the time? In smelly carpet slippers?"

There in front of the mirror stood Roger, and beside him stood somebody else. The small bearded man in the skullcap, who was brushing mirror mica off his sleeves. He tipped his cap to everyone, including the mirror, which bent a gold leaf of its frame at him in grouchy acknowledgment.

"Am I too late, gentlemen? You both look pretty worn out."

"Not all *that* worn out, Mr. Millhorn," said Prospero. "This is Roger Bacon, and I've told him all about you. Let's go down to the kitchen. I want to make some coffee, but there's a cyanide bottle full of Holland gin on my laboratory shelf, unless someone got desperate and drank it."

"I want to go too," said the mirror. "I'll hold my breath if I don't get to go."

"Oh, all right," said Prospero. "Help me carry this thing, Roger. The last time it held its breath we got two hours of 'Overhead the Moon Is Screaming' and bagpipes playing Gregorian chants."

The mirror, which had been made to feel quite important in the last three days—everyone had gone upstairs to look at it and ask it questions—hummed contentedly as the little procession made its way down to the kitchen. They set

it on a chair drawn up to the big white table, and Prospero started to grind up some coffee beans. As he turned the ornate handle of the big walnut grinder, he talked with the other two men.

"Now, Mr. Millhorn. You will hear later what happened to me—the whole thing, before and after I met you—because I insist on your staying several days. Bed and breakfast, you know. But I'm not sure what or who I defeated."

"Neither am I," said Millhorn, "but I'll tell you what happened. We fought for a solid hour. I've never met a magician that strong, and if he had known anything about the Kabbala, we might not be sitting here now. In any case, the local farmers must have thought it was a winter thunderstorm, the way we carried on. Funny thing, though, and you'll have to tell me more about that man. I knew you both were coming, of course. I've known for years through specular stones and certain dark hints in my books, and through dreams. But—"

"Get back to what you were saying," said Prospero, who had stopped turning the grinder. "What do you mean by 'funny thing'?"

"I was getting to that. Well, his mind had a way of coming . . . *unfocused*. That's the only way I can put it. I could feel the force of his spells bursting around me or rushing past me, and once or twice I came close to being destroyed. But his concentration wavered and never built up into the kind of power I knew he could wield. It's a harrowing feeling to face someone you know can kill you if he puts his mind to it. But he didn't put his mind to it. He kept going back to something else that had nothing to do with me. Finally I hit him with a thing I'd never had the courage to use before. It's a long chant, and if you don't get it all out in one breath, it

173

turns on you. A huge red pentacle appeared in the air with an Aleph in the middle of it, and when it burst I was knocked down. When I got up the light was gone. His light, that is, since I never saw any more of him than that yellow lantern glowing at the bottom of the stairs. I clumped out through the snow and found a book lying on the steps. It was open to the last page, and I don't mind telling you I couldn't read a blessed word. At the bottom, though, where the colophon usually is in old books, there was something you would have recognized. Four dolphins in the shape of a cross, the sign of the four elementals, the spirits who were chained centuries ago by wizards whose names are not even known any more. As I stood looking at it, the book appeared to be . . . well . . . *reading itself.* The letters glowed, one after another, and the book gave off such a heat that I couldn't get near it. Then, all of a sudden, it crumpled into a black ball of ashes and sank into the snow. Something was over, and you'll have to tell me what."

He stopped, took a long drink of gin, and went on.

"I do, however, have an idea of what happened to the sorcerer. There is a stone marker, a leaning thing with letters up and down the sides. It's at the crossroads near my house, and it wasn't there before. If you stand next to it you have the feeling that someone is looking at you."

Prospero looked sadly at him. "Yes, I think you're right. You see, the globes always showed . . . "

He was interrupted by a sound like a two-man saw biting into a tree full of nails. The mirror was asleep.

174

AWARD-WINNING

Science Fiction!

The following titles are winners of the prestigious Nebula or Hugo Award for excellence in Science Fiction. A must for lovers of good science fiction everywhere!

☐ 77420-2	**SOLDIER ASK NOT,** Gordon R. Dickson	$2.75
☐ 47809-3	**THE LEFT HAND OF DARKNESS,** Ursula K. LeGuin	$2.95
☐ 06223-7	**THE BIG TIME,** Fritz Leiber	$2.50
☐ 16651-2	**THE DRAGON MASTERS,** Jack Vance	$1.95
☐ 16706-3	**THE DREAM MASTER,** Roger Zelazny	$2.25
☐ 24905-1	**FOUR FOR TOMORROW,** Roger Zelazny	$2.25
☐ 80698-8	**THIS IMMORTAL,** Roger Zelazny	$2.75

Prices may be slightly higher in Canada.

BEST-SELLING

Science Fiction
and
Fantasy

☐ 47809-3	**THE LEFT HAND OF DARKNESS,** Ursula K. LeGuin	$2.95
☐ 16012-3	**DORSAI!,** Gordon R. Dickson	$2.75
☐ 80581-7	**THIEVES' WORLD,** Robert Lynn Asprin, editor	$2.95
☐ 11577-2	**CONAN #1,** Robert E.Howard, L. Sprague de Camp, Lin Carter	$2.50
☐ 49142-1	**LORD DARCY INVESTIGATES,** Randell Garrett	$2.75
☐ 21889-X	**EXPANDED UNIVERSE,** Robert A. Heinlein	$3.95
☐ 87328-6	**THE WARLOCK UNLOCKED,** Christopher Stasheff	$2.95
☐ 26187-6	**FUZZY SAPIENS,** H. Beam Piper	$2.75
☐ 05469-2	**BERSERKER,** Fred Saberhagen	$2.75
☐ 10253-0	**CHANGELING,** Roger Zelazny	$2.95
☐ 51552-5	**THE MAGIC GOES AWAY,** Larry Niven	$2.75

Prices may be slightly higer in Canada.

Available at your local bookstore or return this form to:

ACE SCIENCE FICTION
Book Mailing Service
P.O. Box 690, Rockville Centre, NY 11571

Please send me the titles checked above. I enclose _____ Include 75¢ for postage and handling if one book is ordered; 25¢ per book for two or more not to exceed $1.75. California, Illinois, New York and Tennessee residents please add sales tax.

NAME_____

ADDRESS_____

CITY_____STATE/ZIP_____

(allow six weeks for delivery)   **SF 9**